McCracken and the Lost Oasis

Moving on, we soon found ourselves climbing a gentle incline towards double doors, once more decorated with the phoenix motif. This time, however, the keyhole was well within reach. And the key fitted. I turned it and pushed the doors open.

The inside was dark, but not without light. It entered through a circular vent in the roof. The whole room, in fact, was circular, with ranks of seats around the walls and a raised platform in the middle of it. The light from above lit up the platform, and the throne that stood upon it.

Upon the throne, a figure was seated. The figure wore a crown. A red and gold robe was draped about his shoulders. In one hand was a flail like the ones held by pharaohs.

In the other was the Staff of the Phoenix.

Also by Mark Adderley

The Hawk and the Wolf
The Hawk and the Cup
The Hawk and the Huntress

For Young Readers:
McCracken and the Lost Island
McCracken and the Lost Valley
McCracken and the Lost City
McCracken and the Lost Lagoon
McCracken and the Lost Lady
McCracken and the Lost Cavern

McCracken and the Lost Oasis

By Mark Adderley

Scriptorium Press
Vermillion, South Dakota
2020

Published by Scriptorium Press,
Vermillion, South Dakota

To Christopher James Adderley
Both of Them

Contents

Chapter 1
Danger on the Nile

The gunshot woke me in the small hours of the morning, and for a few moments I could not remember where I was. Moonlight filtered through louvered windows beside my bed, letting barred silver fall across me and my beautiful dark-haired wife Ariadne. Archie lay in his own bed, Rose in her crib. But where was I?

I could hear voices now—too far away to make out words, just a chaotic hubbub really. The air was cool, but that smell of silt . . . what did it mean?

Egypt—that was it! We were in a little two-masted boat, a dahabiyah named the *Ghazal*, anchored a little south of Cairo. We had come to Egypt at the request of a friend of ours, Cristofero di Serpente. Serpe (our friend's nickname) was an Italian archaeologist who had found something mysterious and thought Ari could help him interpret it.

Another gunshot rang out, and I started under the covers, in spite of myself. Ever since the few days I had spent in the trenches, over a year ago now, sharp noises like that had bothered me more than I wanted to admit.

Nevertheless, that was a gunshot I had heard, not a door slamming or a book falling to the floor.

Someone had squeezed a trigger and discharged a bullet.

"Honey?" the sleepy voice of my wife said in her American accent.

"I heard it," I said. "I'll go and investigate."

Swinging my legs out of bed, I threw on some clothes and dashed up the companionway to the upper deck. Hassan Reis, the captain of the *Ghazal*, and Omar, the dragoman we had hired in Cairo, were there, staring out at the landscape that was still dark, for the top rim of the sun had not yet shown itself over the eastern mountains. The crew huddled below, chattering in hushed voices and pointing. Seeing my arrival, Hassan pointed. "Rebels, *effendim*. They want you Britishers to leave, I think."

"Why are they bothering us?" I asked. I had known about the rebels—it was why we had taken a boat from Cairo, rather than driving.

"What's going on, McCracken?" Our traveling companion, an American called Remington Smith, had joined us, dressed in long underwear. There was a surprising steel in his voice, and he clasped a Colt 1911 in his right hand. I indicated that Hassan would answer him, but he seemed preoccupied and Omar explained instead: "These people, most distinguished gentleman, they think they helped the Britishers enough during the war, God be praised it is now over. Now they want the country from the Britishers. They want to rule their own people."

"Isn't that what we all want?" I said.

"Yes, indeed, *Sayyd.*" Omar's voice was low but firm. "You speak the truth."

"What do they want from us?" asked Smith.

Hassan finished his contemplations and turned to the American. "They want me to hand you over to them."

"I'm not British," Smith pointed out with frankness.

Hassan gave a shrug. "They do not care. They are a rabble." As if to confirm his words, another gunshot rang out, and another. I could see the muzzle-flashes on the darkened shore, and they illuminated thick moustaches, bright and angry eyes, and dark turbans. Smith had ducked on hearing the gunshots, but I knew the rebels were too far away to hit anything deliberately with those weapons.

"Surely," Smith bristled, "you don't intend to hand us over?"

"Of course he doesn't," said Ari. She had arrived on the upper deck, Rose in one arm, Archie holding her hand.

Hassan made the salaam, touching his breast, lips and forehead. "My thanks to you, honourable lady. Some captains would do so, of course. But we have a contract. Besides," he waved a dismissive hand towards the rebels on the shore, "these are desert people, they have no honour."

"Some desert people have much honour." Omar's voice had a quiet danger to it.

"My apologies, Omar ibn Mukhdar, you are right. I make this mistake because I am concerned—for my ship and for my passengers."

A voice from the shore shouted something in rapid and rough-sounding Arabic. His words were punctuated by gunshots.

"What did he say?" I asked.

"He wants us to hand over the wealthy Britishers to him." It was Ari who had provided the translation.

"Can't we just leave?" asked Smith. "Just cruise on down the river?"

"Remington-bey," said Hassan gently but firmly, "we could cast off, but still we would move quite slowly." He raised a hand over his head. "You can feel that there is no wind. We would have to pole along the river—very slow at first. This would not take us out of danger."

"What do those men want?" asked Archie.

Smith looked down at him. "They want your Pa," he said.

Archie became fierce. "They can't have him! Dad will shoot them. He'll shoot them all if they try and take him away. My Dad is brave. He won't let them take him!"

I went down on one knee and hugged him. "Of course I won't let them take me away from you," I assured him.

"Shoot them with your gun," advised Archie, with some passion.

"Well, we have to try other things before we start shooting."

"Those bad men are shooting," Archie pointed out, and gunfire crackled on the shore. Archie's expression said, "I told you so."

"They're shooting in the air. So far, they haven't fired at us."

"Daddy's right, sweetheart," said Ari. "We should pray for them."

"We should throw fire at them," Archie said, his fierceness mounting. "That will make them go away."

I suddenly an idea. "Ari," I said, "Would you fetch my Fire Stone, please?"

Ari's brow furrowed slightly, but then light dawned behind her eyes and, passing Rose to me for a moment, she dashed off below to our cabin.

The Fire Stone. It had been important on an adventure that had come to us, before the war. My father had picked it up, many years ago, on his travels through North Africa, at a bazaar in the city of Tripoli. I had thought it had been lost, but then we had asked our friend, Vassily Sikorsky, to send us our things the airship. When, in Cairo, we had opened the boxes Sikorsky had sent, the Fire Stone had been in one of them.

The rabble on the shore were getting louder and louder, the gunshots more frequent, and Archie covered his ears and buried his face in my shoulder. "Tell them to stop, Dad," he pleaded.

"I will. Just wait for Mum to get back." Standing slowly, with Rose in my arms and Archie clinging to my leg, I said to Hassan Reis, "Tell them you have no Britishers aboard. Tell them the Pharaohs are aboard. If they do not stop this rabble-rousing at once, the Pharaoh will awaken and smite them with fire from Heaven."

"Why would I tell them this?" wondered Hassan. His eyes suggested I was insane.

"Just tell them—leave the rest to me."

Hassan gave his characteristic shrug, turned towards the shore and, raising his voice, bellowed a stream of aggressive-sounding Arabic. Some laughter could be heard from the shore, and Hassan repeated himself, louder and more insistent this time. Just as he finished, Ari returned. She handed me the Fire Stone and I handed her Rose.

The orichalcum shone with red fire in the darkness of the Egyptian night

I took from my pocket my electric torch and unscrewed the end; the battery inside jumped out a little, under the pressure of the spring at the negative end.

On the shore, the rabble was getting louder, and the gunshots were a constant crackling, like a battle. "Warn them again, Hassan Reis," I said. "And, kids—watch out. There's going to be a loud noise." Holding the Fire Stone up, I pressed the exposed end of the battery to it.

Immediately, a blinding flash lit up the night, so that we could see the mob on the shore, their shadows sharp and long behind them. A crashing sound, like the explosion of a hand-grenade, broke out, and the smell of ozone filled my nostrils. The rabble fell silent, but there came an uproar from the deck-hands, who threw themselves face-down on the deck. Smith gave a gasp; Hassan cried out in an unexpectedly falsetto voice; Omar flinched, but recovered quickly. Ari retained her calm; she had seen my orichalcum work before. For a moment, we could see nothing, blinded by the flash.

Archie giggled. "That was fun," he commented. "Boom! Do it again, Dad!" And he leaped into the air in imitation of the explosion. I tousled his hair.

Slowly, our eyes re-accustomed themselves to the dark, and then we could make out a crater about eight feet across on the shore, smoke meandering from its lip in little tendrils. The mob was absolutely silent, their eyes wide.

"Oh, very bully, McCracken-bey!" cried Hassan. "You have got them well, effendim!"

Omar made the salaam. "You are El Cracken. You are the one from whose hand springs strength."

"What is it?" Smith's voice was awestruck, his eyes fixed on the Fire Stone.

"Just something my Dad picked up years ago." I dropped the orichalcum and the torch into my pocket.

"Well," remarked Smith, "you seem to have hidden gifts!"

"You've no idea," said Ari, with a laugh.

By now, the natives were slowly draining away from the shore, lit up by the grey light of the dawn.

"All the same," I said to Hassan, "we'd better cast off right away.

Hassan Reis touched his forehead and bellowed out commands to the deck-hands. They started poling us away from the shore.

"I think I'll get some breakfast," announced Smith. "With all this excitement, I don't think I'll be able to sleep! Will you join me, McCracken?"

I shook my head. "Thanks, Smith, but I think I'll keep an eye on things on the shore."

"You do that," said Ari, taking Archie's hand and leading him back down the companionway. "I'm going to try and snatch another hour of sleep before breakfast."

We moored a short distance away, Omar and I remaining on guard, me with my Webley, Omar with a Martini-Henry. But the rebels did not return.

Chapter 2
A Meeting in Egypt

It was a hot afternoon a couple of days later when we stepped off the boat and onto the sands of Elephantine Island, which divided the River Nile at the city of Aswan. Far off, but still in sight, was the magnificent Aswan Dam, completed almost ten years ago now; in the other direction, the wharf gave way to a mix of sand and yellow boulders, then palm groves and cotton fields. Somewhere among them lay Serpe's archaeological dig.

"Isn't this exciting?" enthused Ari. She carried Rose on one hip; Archie sat wriggling on my shoulders.

"I'm glad to have arrived. It's seemed like a long trip from Cairo."

"Not even two weeks," Ari responded to me. "Don't be so impatient. This is the first time in Egypt for Rose and Archie."

"What do you think, old chap?" I looked up at Archie. "Do you want to go and see some more mouldy old ruins, or the bright new shiny dam?"

"Dam dam dam dam dam dam dam," chirped Archie.

Ari clicked her tongue. "Archimedes Edmund," she said, and we could both tell she meant business, "you know you're not supposed to use that word."

I could feel Archie cranking back to argue, and I knew in the deepest part of my soul that it was a dreadfully unwise thing to do; but before the eruption occurred, we all turned on hearing my name called out.

"Macaroni!" Serpe, engineer and antiquarian, was speeding towards us, having just emerged from among the rocks and palm trees. My old college friend wore a grey waistcoat and rolled-up sleeves, and sported a neat little beard. I set Archie down just in time for him to pound me to him in a big hug.

"We are we are we are we are we are the engineers!" he sang, beginning to dance a little jig.

"We can we can we can we can demolish forty beers!" I sang back. And together we finished the verse: "Drink rum drink rum drink rum—"

"Not in front of the children!" Ari broke in upon the joy of our reunion, and we both shut up at once. "Cristofero, how lovely to see you again!"

"Ah, Signora McCracken, how beautiful you continue to be!" They hugged. "And the *bambini*!" enthused Serpe, dropping to his knees to ruffle Archie's hair and kiss Rose's hand as if she were a princess. "Ah, *che bellisimi!*" After the introductions, Serpe went on, "My Maria, she is here also, and our own *bambini*!"

"All of them?"

Serpe gave a shrug. "As many as there are—only eight so far. But one more will be here *prima di Pasqua*."

"One more before Easter!" exclaimed Ari with joy. "Congratulations, Cristofero!"

"Nine is—what is the phrase?—a good beginning." Serpe beamed from ear to ear. "How was your journey?"

"Uneventful," I answered.

"Apart from the crocodile," Ari pointed out. "And the revolutionaries."

"They didn't really slow us down, though, did they?" Turning to Serpe, I changed the subject. "All right, Serpe," I said, "here we are. So what's the big mystery?"

"*Mysterio*?" repeated Serpe. "Macaroni, how is it with you, that everything must be the adventure? I have a little problem, that is all, and I think your gifted wife might be the person who can help me."

I took out a crumpled telegram from my pocket and read it aloud. "PUZZLING DISCOVERY. COME AT ONCE. SERPE."

Serpe waved a forefinger at me. "I send this message over a month ago!" he chided.

"It's not so easy getting around," I protested, "what with the war ending not so long ago. And a dahabiyah . . . " I indicated the boat, admittedly quite lovely, that we had sailed here upon. The masts bobbed a little as the gentle waters of the Nile bore the old-fashioned vessel up and down. "It's not a speedy form of transport."

"No matter," replied Serpe. "You are here and the puzzle is still with us, and I think only Signora Macaroni can help us with it."

"McCracken," I insisted, as I had been insisting for almost twenty years now. "The name's McCracken, not Macaroni."

"*Si*, is what I say, Macaroni." His eye glinted. "Now, what is it you would wish to do? Do you wish to rest? Have a drink? Or can we go right to the heart of this *mysterio*?" He crooked a finger. "*Andiamo!*"

After a few turns among yellow rocks, we came to the dig. Having been funded by the Pontifical Institute of Rome, it was covered with priests and brothers of the Jesuit order, some kneeling on planks of wood with their brushes and trowels, others sketching their findings.

"This is first of all the site of temples to Khnum and Satis, god and goddess of the Nile, but in the sixth century BC, there was a most curious settlement here." He stopped and indicated some low walls enclosing a spacious courtyard with a building roughly in the centre of it. "Do you know what this is, Signora?"

Ari entered the enclosure and walked about, examining the walls, scanning the courtyard for its dimensions. The children followed her, and Archie began climbing the walls and walking along the tops of them, his arms out for balance.

Ari looked puzzled. "This is not Egyptian," she said. "If I weren't here, I'd say . . . "

Serpe was smiling broadly, his eyes afire. "Continue, Signora. If it were not that you were in Egypt?"

"Well, it's much smaller, of course, but it reminds me of the temple in Jerusalem. The wide courtyard, the shape of the building in the centre. But it isn't possible, is it?"

Serpe nodded with enthusiasm. "*Si*, Signora, it is possible! We have discovered here many letters, written on papyrus in the language *Ebraico*."

"In Hebrew?"

"That is correct!" Serpe gave a nod. "An Israelite garrison, with their families, settled here in the sixth century—at the time of the Captivity of Babylon."

"Well," said Ari, "that is a mystery, all right." She looked a little confused, and I knew she was trying to figure out why Serpe had expected her to be able to offer any solution to this puzzle. It seemed to have been solved already.

Serpe gave us his most charming smile. "But, as you have probably guessed, that is not the surprise for which I summon you here," he said. "For that, you must come with me now."

"Where are we going?" I asked.

"To the Artifact Room," he said.

Serpe led us out of the temple and into the street. Before we had gone far, we saw one of the Jesuits, in his late thirties with a mop of curly black hair, pushing a wheelbarrow along the street towards us. On seeing Serpe, his face split into a good-natured grin and he set down his wheelbarrow.

"Top of the morning to you, Mr. Serpente," he beamed.

"Fr. Murphy, allow me to introduce you to my very good *amico*, Mac-Cracken, and his wife, Ariadne."

"Father Eoghan Murphy," said the priest, shaking hands with each of us in turn. "Let's see now. We have an Irishman, a Scotsman, a score or two Italians, and I assume you are an American, isn't that right, Mrs. McCracken?"

Ari confirmed the rumours he had heard.

"And Miss Fortescue is an Englishwoman," Serpe observed.

"Well, God save her, we shan't hold that against her, since she's also a true daughter of the universal Church. We'll have a veritable League of Nations here in Aswan if we don't look out."

"Who is this Fortescue?" I asked.

"A bit of an adventuress, if you ask me," answered Fr. Murphy. "She's been traveling of late—China, Bangkok, South America and so forth, but she's English and, what's more, Catholic, and an Egyptologist to boot, which is what brought her here. And who is this fine young man?" Fr. Murphy went down on one knee so that his head was level with Archie's. I introduced Archie and Rose. "Why, doesn't he look strong enough to carry all this load I'm taking to the Artifact House by himself?"

"Padre Murfeo," said Serpe, "if we were to take this load of things to the Artifact House, could you take the *bambini* to Maria? She is with our *bambini* on the *piscina*."

"Well," said Fr. Murphy dubiously, "I don't know if this serious young man is the beach-going type. I don't know he'd enjoy playing with the other children on the beach, now."

"I would, though," Archie assured him. We arranged for Fr. Murphy to take Rose and Archie, then Ari and I followed Serpe, trundling the wheelbarrow along, through the streets of the ancient city.

A short time later, we found ourselves outside a large stone house in the Nubian style, its mud-coloured walls daubed with rows and rows of pictures of birds and trees. Serpe unlocked the green door and led us inside.

It took a few moments for our eyes to adjust to the difference in light. But then we could see a spacious room with whitewashed walls, comfortable-looking wicker chairs, and a couple of rough-hewn but very lovely tables. Shelves had been improvised from planks and bricks, and upon these rested the various broken pieces of pottery and metal recovered from the dig. In the far corner, solid and heavy and glossy with dark green paint, was the kind of safe that every outlaw in the American West just itched to blow up. Serpe strode right up to it, spun the combination lock back and forth, and threw open the door. He took out a stack of ancient papyrus manuscripts and set them on one of the tables.

"These pages," explained Serpe, "they were all found in one chest, and in this order, so I am very careful, you see, to leave the order undisturbed while I look through them. Most of them are papyrus, but this one, the only one sewn together into a codex, a book, is not papyrus, but *pergamena—como se dice in Inglese?*"

"Parchment," said Ari.

"*Si, parch-a-mente.*"

Ari saw that this was giving me some difficulty, so she explained. "The difference, honey, is that papyrus, which is made from a plant that grows in Egypt, was mostly used in north Africa, whereas parchment, which is made from the skin of a calf, was more common throughout Europe."

"This papyrus, it is very, very old," put in Serpe. "The Egyptian scribes, they finished using papyrus two centuries before the birth of Our Lord."

"So," concluded Ari, "whereas the papyrus must have been put here many centuries before Christ, the parchment suggests a much later date—perhaps as late as the Middle Ages. Why was a later manuscript discovered among all these more ancient documents? It's an anomaly."

"All these Hebrew papyri," went on Serpe, "they are letters, of great interest to historians. They describe the marriages of the Hebrew people here, what they buy and sell, who owed money to whom and how much. But this one—ah!" He held up the codex and handed it to Ari. I frowned. I had expected some ornate kind of Gothic script, or perhaps Arabic, but this was neither. There were many curls like commas, large dots and circles and bold vertical slashes. To me, it was completely incomprehensible.

But not to Ari. "It looks like Tifinagh," she announced. "See those dots arranged in a triangle? Those indicate the beginning of a sentence."

"I've never heard of Tifinagh," I said. "What is it?"

"It's an alphabet, rather than a language," replied Ari, "The parchment looks medieval, probably no earlier than twelfth century, but no later than the fifteenth. So the language will probably be a dialect of Old Berber, I shouldn't wonder. Do you have any reference books?"

"Alas, *signora*, no. But there is an excellent library in Aswan. You are very likely to find what you seek there."

"I'll look on Monday; tomorrow is Sunday, and there will be Mass. Can I spend some time with the codex today? I'd like to copy out some passages, so I don't have to take it away."

"But of course, *signora*!" exclaimed Serpe, and it was settled.

Serpe and I wandered down to the shoreline, but before we reached the river, I could already hear the sound of delighted children at play. Then, surmounting the sand-dunes on the edge of the beach, I saw the children running up and down the sand, and Fr. Murphy dashing back and forth with them. Archie was among them, but not Rose. It took a moment to locate her, asleep on a large bath-towel, in the shade of an umbrella. Beside her slumbered a couple of Serpe's younger children. Sitting with them, watching the children at play, was Maria, Serpe's wife.

Seeing their father, Serpe's children ran to greet him, wrapping themselves around his knees in a joyful, squealing mass. Archie came with them, Fr. Murphy following more slowly

Maria gave me a radiant smile. "Signor McCracken, how wonderful to see you again! Always, my husband speaks of wishing to see you again, and perhaps to ride in the *dirigibile*!"

"Maria!" I stooped to kiss her hand. "I don't think we've met since before the war. Sorry, but Sikorsky has the airship right now—he and Fritz are attempting to find their families in Germany and Russia. But they'll be joining us here soon."

"I am certain Cristofero will be delighted by that."

I shot a glance at my friend. "Thanks for looking after old Serpe, Maria—he doesn't do a very good job of it himself."

She smiled again, then turned to her husband. "Please give this to Elena," she said, handing him a small bottle of medicine. "She would not take it from me."

"Elena," chided Serpe, "why will you not take your medicine from Mama?"

The girl did not look ashamed; in fact, she looked positive she could easily bend her father to her will. She said something in Italian, but Serpe held up his hand to silence her. "No, my dear. We must speak English when we have English visitors." He shook a pill out of the bottle and held it up.

"Open your mouth and think of England," I advised Elena, "or, better still, Scotland."

Serpe's eyes twinkled. "Open your mouth, Elena, and think of *Roma*!"

"Open your mouth and think of eyeball soup," put in one of Serpe's boys unpredictably.

"I will open my mouth and think of *Jesus*!" announced Elena, closing her eyes and opening her mouth wide.

"Elena is correct!" declared Serpe, softly closing her lips over the medicine. "Who will protect us from sickness better than Our Lord, eh?" Beaming down at Elena, he planted a kiss on the top of her head. "Ah, *che bellisima!* What a beautiful thing is the faith of children!"

One of Serpe's girls stepped up to Fr. Murphy and said something in Italian, concluding, "*Padre Murfeo, per favo-o-ore!*" Smiling, Fr. Murphy said, "Well, aren't you just the sweetest little colleen I ever did see outside of good old Killarney itself? Of course I'll play Italian Bulldogs with you, though if you'll excuse me, I need to rest a little while first. Why don't you play by yourselves a bit, and I'll join you after I've got my breath back? Don't run out of sight, now! I have to warn you all, I saw a great big crocodile in the reeds down there yesterday."

"Oh, my Dad can kill crocodiles just with his hands," Archie assured them, in an off-hand way.

All eyes turned on me. There were coo's of admiration from the children.

Blushing, I said, "Well, it's not so difficult, once you get past the teeth, Anyway, Archie, it was Mr. Omar who really killed the crocodile, not your Dad."

Archie shrugged, as if such details were too pettifogging for his serious consideration.

Turning to the children, Archie said, "Let's play St. George and the Crocodile. I'm St. George!" And off they ran to the edge of the water.

As Serpe and Maria started playing with one of the babies, who had just woken up, I observed, "You seem to be very popular with the children, Fr. Murphy."

"Praised be God," replied Fr. Murphy, crossing himself, "it's a gift He has granted me in His wisdom. And you, Mr. McCracken—I gather you have a number of gifts yourself, even laying aside the slaying of crocodiles."

"As you say," I answered him, "gifts that God gives. Anyway, my wife is the truly gifted one. It's her skills that are in demand here."

"Not all adventures involve shooting and chasing, though, Mr. McCracken, wouldn't you say?"

"I'm sure you're right, Father," I answered. "But I prefer that type of adventure myself."

Fr. Murphy's eyes seemed to bore deeply into me for a few moments, then they slid away to watch the children. "I'd say one of your gifts, Mr. McCracken, is the sacrifice of fatherhood. Your boy is a bright little spark, and a faithful follower of Our Lord. He does you great credit. And then there's the little girl. It's a very limited concept of adventure that claims that having a family is of slight importance."

I blushed again, but could find nothing to say.

Fr. Murphy pushed himself to his feet. "Mrs. McCracken, so nice to see you again!"

Turning, I saw Ari approaching, a sheaf of papers in the crook of her arm, her eyes bright in the shadow of her hat's wide brim. She took a moment to check on Rose and locate Archie among the knot of yelling children.

"Fr. Murphy," said Ari, "perhaps you can help us. We were looking for a place to go for Mass tomorrow?"

"Ah now, there you strike me in the place closest to my heart, do you not! Well, if there isn't a little Nubian village not far from here, called Koti, where there's a ramshackle little Coptic Church, struggling to survive among all the mosques, and don't they let an Irish Jesuit celebrate the Holy Sacrifice of the Mass there once a week, bless their hearts?"

"Thank you, Father," said Ari. "We'll see you in the morning."

"Ten o'clock sharp." Fr. Murphy paused a moment. "And see if I don't introduce you to an interesting fellow by the name of Digger Dawkins—an Australian, wouldn't you know it, just to expand the international flavour of our little community here. I think you'll enjoy talking to him, so you will. Now, if you'll excuse me, I promised a game of Italian Bulldogs to the budding adults over there." And he left us to play with the children.

CHAPTER 3
DIGGER

The next day, Serpe led us to the village of Koti, where we found the chapel Fr. Murphy had described to us. On either side of the dark wooden doors rose a domed tower with mud-brick walls. Inside, the reredos and icons reminded me of Russian orthodox churches. The scent of incense hung upon the air.

Shortly after we had sat down, a blond-haired man genuflected and took a seat across the aisle from us. He placed a slouch hat on the pew beside him, then went to his knees in prayer. His face, arms and knees were deeply suntanned.

"Daddy," Archie whispered, somewhat more loudly than made me comfortable, "that man is wearing shorts." He sounded scandalized.

"That doesn't mean you can," I answered. "You're under my authority, and I say you wear your Sunday Best to Mass."

"Whose authority is *he* under?" wondered Archie, eyeing the newcomer enviously.

"Perhaps his Mommy's," whispered Ari.

Archie clearly didn't buy it, but it hardly mattered, as then the bell rang and Fr. Murphy processed in with a pair of grinning altar-boys.

As we filed out after Mass, Fr. Murphy beckoned us over and introduced us to the individual whose Sunday Best had so horrified Archie.

"Mr. and Mrs. McCracken, allow me to introduce you to Australia's finest, Digory Dawkins."

"G'day," said the Australian, extending his hand to each of us in turn. "Damned stupid name, isn't it? Excuse my language, but it is."

"It's nice to meet you, Mr. Dawkins," said Ari.

Digger scratched the back of his head with the hand that wasn't holding his almost entirely shapeless hat. He made a grimace. "Yeah, perhaps you can call me Digger. Had a sheila once who used to take the . . . well, liberties with my name, you might say."

"Used to?" I asked. So many people had been lost in the war, I thought. "Is she all right?"

"I suppose she is," answered Digger. "Ran off with a sheikh, poor girl. Wasn't her fault, she thought I was dead. Poor Barbs."

"Thought you were dead?"

"That's the ticket. Thought I was dead. I nearly bl . . . bloomin' was, too, pardon my French."

"You were missing in action," deduced Ari.

"You got it." Snapping to attention, Digger gave us a smart salute. "Sergeant Digory Dawkins, First Light Car Patrol, at your service."

"I've never heard of the Light Car Patrol," I said, deeply interested.

"New idea—mechanized warfare. Joined up in '16, thinking I could get back at the enemy for Gallipoli, though between you, me, and the dingoes, the real enemy was the British officers who came up with that hare-brained plan. Anyway, they posted me to Cairo instead. The Turks wanted to take the Suez Canal, so they stirred up some local tribesmen, the Senussi, against His Majesty's lawful government in Egypt, and we were assigned to fight them. So we drove our Model-T trucks out into the desert and fought against the little . . . er . . . Arabic fellers, if you'll excuse my language. Anyhow, one day we got ambushed, and when I fell out of my truck, I hit my head on a rock and passed out. I woke up and it was darker than the inside of a dingo's . . . er . . . nose, I reckon, pardon me for saying so, and colder than a stubby fresh out of the cooler, not that I over-indulge in such things, just take a quick coldie now and then. So there I was, gone walkabout in the middle of the North African Outback. It took me almost a month to get back to Cairo, and then I find out my unit's shipped out for Palestine and I'm listed as missing in action, presumed dead."

"And Barbara went with your unit?" Ari was confused.

"Nah, poor girl. She came to Aswan, and I followed her here, but she'd already married the sheikh and moved on. I guess that's a step up from a sergeant. Not her fault, poor Barbs."

“What do you do here, Digger?” asked Ari.

“I work in a mechanic’s shop, fixing automobiles and trucks, like the ones we used in the war. It’s hard yakka, but it pays well. As soon as I’ve saved up the dosh, I’ll be out of here and back to my rellies in Darwin quicker than sh . . . manure off a greased shovel. Pardon the language, ma’am.”

“Why aren’t you wearing your Sunday Best?” demanded Archie disapprovingly.

“Well, these togs *are* my Sunday Best, mate.” Plucking at his shirt, Digger went on, “This is my best flannie. If I had better clothes, you bet I’d wear ’em, just to get His Lordship all stoked up about me. Always pays to get Him Upstairs on your side. It’d be ripper if I had togs like yours. Can I borrow them next week?”

Archie giggled. “They wouldn’t fit you.”

“I’d be rapt if I had a pair of daks like them you’re wearing, mate. Next time I want to impress a sheila, I’m going to ask you to lend me those.”

“Don’t be silly,” said Archie.

“No wukka, mate. Just saying, I think I’d be right dapper, strutting around in them daks. You sure I can’t borrow them?”

“Daddy!” sniggered Archie.

“Don’t worry, Archie,” I said, picking him up, “I won’t let Mr. Dawkins steal your trousers; you can wear them to Mass next week, I promise.” I winked at Digger, who winked back at Archie.

We left Digger with an invitation to dinner later in the week and went back to the *Ghazal*, where Omar had fixed us drinks and *hors d'oeuvres*. Serpe and his family joined us on the *Ghazal*, and we spent the afternoon sipping cool drinks and watching the children play.

The next day, I found Ari had risen before me and she spun round from the mirror with a beaming smile and asked, "How do I look?"

She was dressed in a white shirt with faint pinstripes, accentuated by a black necktie scarf. The tan skirt was cinched at her slender waist, and she had pulled the dark piles of her hair back into a loose bun, so that the early morning sunlight lay softly across her cheek. The deep brown eyes sparkled, and her lips shone.

"Er . . . dressed for the library," I said. "It makes me wish I was a librarian."

After we had enjoyed a leisurely breakfast of coffee, eggs cooked in ghee with dried beef, and a delicious Egyptian flatbread that Omar called *baladi*, drizzled with a tangy tahini sauce, Ari left for the library.

I was at loose ends.

Omar had taken charge of the kids, so I wandered about the archaeological dig, hoping to bump into someone I knew—Fr. Murphy or Serpe. I had seen neither of them, after walking around for almost half an hour, when I stopped in my tracks.

There, squatting on all fours, dusting away at the dirt and occasionally prodding it with a trowel, was a woman in a khaki dress and white pith helmet. She was the only archaeologist I had seen in Elephantine, other than Serpe, who was not a Jesuit. Fr. Murphy had mentioned her. What was her name? I racked my brains, but could come up with nothing. I was about to sneak away so I wouldn't have to confront my failure to remember the lady's name, but as I took a step, I dislodged a rock, which rattled against the stony ground. The woman gave a start totally out of proportion to the noise and turned round. She looked like she had been scared out of her wits: her eyes were wide, her mouth forming a perfect O. Scrambling to her feet, she dusted sand from her skirt.

"I'm sorry, I didn't mean to startle you," I said.

"Oh, that's all right," she replied. When she smiled, I saw that her teeth must have been quite a lot longer than usual, though straight and white. "I was miles away; I'm not usually startled like that." Taking a step forward, she narrowed her eyes and added, "I say, are you McCracken? I've heard of you—Cristofero's been talking about you for weeks now."

"Yes, I am."

"Jolly nice to meet you!" she enthused, shaking my hand vigorously. "My name's Fortescue—Ramona Fortescue. So, you're McCracken, what.

Engineer, adventurer, Papist—the man with a gun in one hand, a rosary in the other, and a slide-rule in the back-pocket."

"I hear you're a Catholic yourself, Miss Fortescue," I said, retrieving my hand and flexing my fingers a little.

"That's the Spanish side of the family—Mama's side," said Ramona. "Gave me m' faith and m' Christian name. 'Fraid it doesn't make me very popular back in Blighty, what."

"That it doesn't," I answered with feeling. "If ever I do anything impressive, people are surprised, like they don't expect much from a Catholic."

There was one of those pauses that often seem awkward, during which Ramona seemed to examine me very closely, as if I were an artifact to be classified.

"Well, I suppose we'll be seeing you quite frequently," I said. "Perhaps you could come to dinner on the *Ghazal* sometime?"

"That would be spiffing!" she replied. "How awfully kind of you—I'd be delighted."

But to my surprise, when I sent Omar to seek her out, he couldn't find her. The days passed, and I forgot about Ramona Fortescue, English Catholic archaeologist. Fr. Murphy expressed his surprise and concern that she seemed to have disappeared from the dig. The meeting remained a curious, unexplained event slowly fading from my memory, and

I thought that we had seen the last of Miss Fortescue, and that her importance to what we were doing at Elephantine was probably about as close to nil as could be imagined.

But I was wrong on both counts.

The highlight of the next few days was taking Archie to visit the dam, just a few miles south of Elephantine. It was almost ten years old now, a wonder of modern engineering, its buttresses and sluice gates rising majestically above the gently inclined heads of the palm trees that proliferated at its foot like worshipers. Archie was suitably appreciative, though he grew impatient far sooner than I did, and I could have seen a lot more of it when it was time to return to the *Ghazal*.

For a week, I saw almost nothing of Ari. She would leave in the morning and return in the late afternoon, sometimes later, after Archie and Rose were in bed. On Saturday, Digger arrived for dinner, and Ari still wasn't back. She arrived barely in time for Grace, setting her satchel on a side-table to pray with us.

Omar had excelled himself. In the middle of the mahogany table were bowls containing falafel, pickled cucumbers and onions, couscous, green beans and onions in a spicy red sauce, and long sausages made from minced beef and onions, and flavoured with oregano, that Omar called *kofta*. Spaced around the table were little bowls of olive oil and of *dukka*, a blend of spices that was hot but very tasty. The aroma of oregano, mixed with cumin, garlic and onion, hung delightfully on the air.

After we had finished praising Omar for his culinary skills and eaten in appreciative silence for a few moments, Fr. Murphy said, "So, Mrs. McCracken, don't be keeping us in suspense, now. What have you discovered about that mysterious manuscript?"

Ari set down her knife and fork, picked up a piece of pita bread and held it contemplatively for a moment. "I haven't translated any of it yet, but I know a lot more about it." She dipped the bread into some olive oil, and then into the dukka, and popped it into her mouth. After a moment, she swallowed and went on, "I haven't quite identified the principle language in which it's written—it's not a dialect of Berber at all, which is what I'd suspected. It looks like a Saharan language, perhaps from southwestern Cyrenaica or southeastern Fezzan. There are a lot in that area—Tedaga, Dazaga, Kanuri, Kanembu, Zaghawa, Berti . . . but oddly enough, there are some words in it obviously derived from Latin and French."

"*Latino e Francese!*" Serpe was taken aback.

"Yes, I thought that was strange. The second word in the manuscript is *Deus*, *God*, and a little later on *Solfitor*."

"*Salvator*?" Serpe's eyes were narrowed. "Saviour?"

"I think so. Then there are words like *honestet* and *messire*, which are Old French words meaning *honour* and *sir*. Sometimes, you'll see *messire*, sometimes the Latin *dominus*. And there are personal names. I've seen Bohemund and Artaud."

"French names," said Fr. Murphy. "This *is* a mystery!"

"They sound like Crusaders or something," Digger observed.

"Bohemund was the name of one of the leaders of the First Crusade in 1099," explained Ari. "When Jerusalem had been captured, he made himself Prince of Antioch. But it was a fairly common name. Another name I saw didn't sound either French or Latin." Ari paused. "It looks like *Zerzura*."

Two people in the room gave a visible start at the mention of the word. One was Omar, who looked up abruptly and stared at us with his dark, intense eyes; the second was Digger, who said, "Strewth! I've seen that word before." Delving into the inside pocket of his "flannie," he produced a crumpled piece of paper, scrawled with a childish handwriting. "Ah, here it is—my last letter from Barbs, poor girl." He cleared his throat. "*My Dear Darling*—she used to call me that all the time, like it was my name or something—*My Dear Darling, I'm right sorry to have to tell you this, especially since I think you might be dead by now, but I can't be your sheila no more. A very nice bloke, who calls himself the Sheikh of Zerzura, has offered to marry me, and I'm inclined to accept his offer. Yours in love for ever, Barbs. P. S. The Sheikh tells me he likes blondes; pray he don't find out I'm really a red-head.*"

"Zerzura!" Fr. Murphy sat back in his chair, cradling a cup of tea. "What a fanciful name! Where could it be, I wonder?"

"It is nowhere," said a voice. We all turned around to see that it was Omar who had spoken. He stepped around from behind the bar and inclined his head in a respectful bow. "This is not a real place, but a place of legend, a myth. It is a story the mothers of my people tell their children at night, when they wish them to sleep happily."

"But what *is* it?" I asked.

"Zerzura is the lost oasis," explained Omar. "It is a place of green trees and blue pools, with luscious grass, where the fortunate sojourner may eat the dates and drink the coconut milk all day. My mother told me that long ago, many hundreds of years, the Tebu people built a white city there among the pools, a city full of gold, with heaps of gemstones, red and blue and green."

"And that's where Barbs went with her sheikh?" said Digger incredulously.

"That is where this person *says* he takes her, effendim," replied Omar. "But there are many men who would claim to be the Sheikh of Zerzura to marry a woman with golden hair."

Digger's grin split his face from ear to ear. "Now *there's* grounds for annulment!" he exclaimed.

Omar reverently made the Salaam. "Your lordships must pardon me for speaking when I should have been silent—that has ever been my way! The women's tales of my people are of little worth."

"I'm not sure they're worthless," replied Ari. "The Tebu people are still around. They're nomads now. If I can find out what language they speak today, that will bring me a little closer to discovering the language of the manuscript. Do you know anything else about this Zerzura place?"

"Your honourable ladyship has plumbed the very depth of your servant's knowledge in this matter," replied Omar who, with a low bow, returned to his place behind the bar.

"Well!" Ari smiled broadly as she picked up her fork and speared a piece of curried lamb. "I feel like I'm much closer to translating this manuscript now."

* * *

Once again, Ari virtually disappeared from our lives for a while, except when she got back from the library. A week went by, and then almost another week, and then one afternoon she hurried somewhat furtively up the gangplank, and in a moment joined me on the upper deck.

I rose to my feet, beginning to frown. "Are you all right?" I asked.

"No, I'm not," returned Ari. She looked left and right. No one else was around. "Can we talk? In the cabin. Where are the children?"

"With Maria." Without another word, we went down the companionway and in a few steps had entered our cabin.

Ari turned the key and shut the window, then sat down and drew a stack of papers out of her bag. "I've translated it," she announced, but quietly.

"That's wonderful!" I declared.

"Yes—and no." She took a deep breath. "It took me a long time because, although Omar was right, the language of the manuscript was an old form of Dazaga, spoken today by the Tebu, it's full of loan-words from French and Latin—the writer uses Latin words for religious ideas, French for ideas relating to food, the household, and war."

There was silence for a moment. I cleared my throat. "Sweetheart," I said, "you're talking like a professor again."

Ari pressed her eyes together for a moment, then opened them and said, "Sorry. I guess I've been alone in the library too long." She gave me a lop-sided smile and then continued, more slowly this time. "I didn't understand either, at first. But it's quite simple. The manuscript was written by a man called Bohemund, who died about 1484. Although his native language was Dazaga, he was descended from Frankish crusaders, and he retained a lot of their words, which have no equivalents in Dazaga. He calls himself the Steward of Zerzura."

"All right. So, where is Zerzura, and who is Bohemund?"

Ari looked up from her papers. Her eyes were almost tearful, so great was her anxiety. "He was a descendant of Artaud, a knight who accompanied King St. Louis on the Seventh Crusade in 1248. Artaud and his eleven companions were shipwrecked, captured, and enslaved by the Tebu, who forced them to build the Shining City in the Oasis of Zerzura." Ari leafed through a few of her papers. "It's a long story, but in the end, the twelve companions were freed by their Tebu masters, and Artaud and his descendants became the Stewards of the Shining City of Zerzura. In the end, the City was destroyed."

"How?"

"It was discovered and attacked by an army led by the Emir of Barqua, a city in Cyrenaica. I think it's Benghazi." Ari took a deep breath. "But the Zerzurans used a terrible weapon on the Emir's army. Here's how Bohemund describes what happened: 'The writer of this history took the Staff of the Phoenix and held it out towards the enemies of Zerzura. And fire flashed forth, and scorched the outsiders, and the walls shook, and rocks from the mountaintops fell upon the city, and many, both friend and foe, fell dead in the streets.' When the dust cleared, Bohemund found that fewer than two-score Zerzurans had survived."

"What did they do?"

"They trekked across the desert, until they came to a place they call Abw—that's Elephantine, here. And here Bohemund died and was buried with the three-lobed key to the King's Chamber and a map showing the location of Zerzura."

"Then let's go and find it!" I cried. "This is the kind of adventure I'm used to!"

Ari wrung her hands. "Do we have to?" she said. "Where is it written that we have to accept every adventure that comes to us? This Staff of the Phoenix can destroy a whole city and most of its population. Can you imagine it in the hands of someone like the Kaiser, or this Mussolini man in Italy? We've just finished one war; must we have another, with even more destructive weapons?"

"But what else can we do? If we find this Phoenix Staff, we control who has access to it."

"Mac, think about it. You've heard of this Mussolini, haven't you? He's already looking for what he calls *vital space*, extra lands he can conquer. Cyrenaica is one of those places. If he turned up with an army, could we really resist him? Even if the Phoenix Staff could kill half his army, he'd seize it with the other half."

I snapped my fingers. "Sir Mansfield Cumming!" I said. "You remember him? He heads up the Secret Service Bureau in England. He'd know what to do. I'll cable him, first thing tomorrow."

"Until then, what do we do?" Ari looked as if she were about to cry, and I leaped to her side and drew her close to me. "I suppose I can . . . I can . . . pretend . . . I'm still . . . still having trouble . . . translating the manuscript . . . perhaps people will believe me . . . "

"My love," I said, quietly in her ear, "don't worry. You won't have to lie. God will send you the words you need. And I'm with you." I could feel her fingers, sharp in my back.

Suddenly, I felt her tense in my arms. "What was that noise?" she asked.

"I didn't hear anything." Nevertheless, I pulled open the door and looked outside. No one was there.

"Was anybody listening to us?" asked Ari.

I shook my head. "I think we're just imagining things because we're tense. All the same, we have to keep that manuscript safe, and get back to England with it; and in the meanwhile, we have to work out what to tell everybody else."

And that's where we left the matter until the following morning.

Chapter 4
The Temple in the Lake

We had resolved to inform everyone that we needed to take the manuscript back to England to get a professional translation, which was certainly our intention.

When we had explained this, over breakfast, Serpe said, "I understand, Signora, but I would still like to see what you have completed so far."

"Well, I haven't really finished my work," said Ari, flushing. "It's a little rough . . . "

"Perhaps," persisted Serpe, "I can help you."

"Perhaps you can," said Ari.

"Is it on board? Is it possible I could look at it now?"

"I'll . . . go and get it." Ari's reluctance was pretty clear. The chair-legs scraped on the floor as she rose, but before she could leave, Fr. Murphy appeared in the doorway.

"God bless all here," he said. Behind him was a man in his mid-thirties, wearing a tan suit and a panama hat. "This gentleman is from Chicago, in America, and he has asked if he might talk to you all. He's a private detective."

The man stepped forward into the saloon, tipping his hat. "The name's Chesterton Valparaiso," he said. "I'm investigating a certain lady who goes by the name of Ramona Fortescue."

"I haven't seen her in a couple of weeks," I said. "I can't even properly remember what she looks like."

"This kid has more disguises than an aging actor, and a different name to go with each one." Reaching into his pocket, Valparaiso took out some cigarette papers and a pouch of tobacco. He began rolling a cigarette, talking while he did it. "Yeah, this gal's had a lot of names—she was Harriet Legendre in Shanghai, when she stole the Golden Lion of the T'ang from the private collection of a Mr. Cheng. Before that, she was Gertrude Dannenborg when she snatched the Sun of the Pacific from the Amalienborg Museum in Copenhagen. She posed as Cassandra Kleftis, the secretary to the Greek shipping tycoon Stasos Aristophanes, so she could steal his cufflinks, valued at almost a quarter million US dollars. She's what you might call an international jewel thief. Her real name is Bevan, Assumpta Bevan."

If someone had thrown a mongoose into a pit of cobras, he could not have expected a more clamorous response than Valparaiso got from his announcement.

"It seems I came to the right place," Valparaiso remarked. "You know this dame?"

"We do," I replied. "Assumpta was a friend of ours, when we were traveling in West Africa a few years ago. She used us as cover to escape from the British Honduras, where she'd stolen a golden idol."

Valparaiso nodded and gave a pert smile. "We got a file on that one," he said. "In fact, we got a file on most of her jobs—two or three a year since '14 at least. She got on the wrong side of a millionaire in Chicago by taking a stroll down the street with his favourite Rubens."

"I haven't read of the disappearance of any Rubens," said Ari.

"No, because it turned up again in an apartment in Manhattan. The cops stopped by after an anonymous tip-off. She didn't get away with that one."

"So why did the millionaire get annoyed?"

"She got into his house and out again without tripping a single alarm. That kind of thing tends to alienate your Chicago millionaire—he paid a large portion of his fortune to protect the rest of it." Valparaiso wagged his still unlit cigarette at us and went on, "I was on security, and I was the guy he tapped to find her, on account of my having worked for Pinkerton's before the war."

I weighed in on the conversation. "I'm not sure she meant to get away with it. Assumpta enjoys the thrill of committing the crime, but she often returns what she steals. She did with the idol."

"That's her game, all right—I guess she gets a kind of a thrill off the danger. Probably the youngest kid—perhaps only kid—of South American money.

She gets bored, so she steals. Finds she likes it, likes the buzz it gives her. So she steals more. She doesn't want the goods. She wants the danger. Gets drunk on it, like the chicken that goes back to the grain trough once too often." He stubbed out his cigarette.

He had not drawn on it even once. The unburned tobacco lay there on the floor, doing nothing, having done nothing.

"Is there something valuable here," Valparaiso asked, "something she might have been after?"

Ari and I exchanged glances. Ari said, "There's the manuscript I'm translating."

"Would you mind fetching it, ma'am?"

"I was about to anyway," answered Ari, and she left the room for a moment.

"It's a strange thing," said Fr. Murphy, shaking his head, "but one of our brothers has disappeared as well—one Brother Osvaldo. Came here with all the right introductions, but nobody knew him. Kept to himself the whole time he was here and then, a few days ago . . . "

The door of the saloon crashed open, interrupting Fr. Murphy's sentence, and Ari stood there, her face white. "It's gone," she said. "Everything is gone—the translation, my notes, everything."

There was stunned silence in the saloon. Valparaiso looked from one to the other of us. "Okay, time you guys came clean," he said. "Tell me the whole story, and don't leave nothing out—every detail might be important."

We told him everything—why we had come to Elephantine, everything Ari could remember about the manuscript she was translating. It took quite a while, and Valparaiso took almost a whole notebook of notes while we talked. In the end, he lowered the notebook and said, "This whole business stinks like San Francisco Harbour at low tide." Turning to Ari, who sat with her face in her hands, he said, "Let me get this straight, you translated the manuscript to the end, but then decided it was too dangerous. So you wanted to take it back, to this . . . " He consulted his notes. "This Mansfield Cumming."

Ari nodded. "And now Assumpta has it—and what she means to do with it, I can't even begin to imagine."

"Were there any clues about this medieval mercenary—what was his name?"

"Bohemund."

"Sure, that guy. Were there any clues as to where he might have hidden this staff, this secret weapon?"

"He hid it in the King's Chamber in Zerzura," answered Ari. "He locked the doors of the chamber and brought the key with him. According to Vernas who wrote the manuscript, Bohemund was buried with the three-lobed key, and with a map to Zerzura."

"Easy!" I declared. "We find Bohemund's tomb, get the key and the map, find Zerzura, and take the Staff before Assumpta gets there."

"Signora, do you remember any more of the manuscript?" asked Serpe.

Ari closed her eyes and, after a moment, recited: "Insert the Key of Zerzura into the Beak of the Phoenix, and the gates of the city will open, which otherwise shall open for no man."

"What about Bohemund's tomb?"

"He's buried in a church on an island above the Cataract."

"That is south from here," explained Serpe. "The people who live on the Nile, they talk of *south* as *up*. The Cataract, it does not exist any more. When they build the dam, nearly ten years ago, the Cataract disappeared as the waters gathered behind the dam. Now there is one great lake and many islands within it. This church may be underwater entirely."

"There's more information," said Ari, her eyes still pressed shut. "It's between two other tombs—of Isis and Augustus, emperor of Rome."

"Isis is a goddess," observed Serpe. "Perhaps he is meaning *temple*. But Augustus, he is buried in Rome. It is possible that Bohemund means *temple* there too."

"Only the sun of noon can reveal him now," said Ari. She opened her eyes. "That's something else from the manuscript: 'Only the sun of noon can reveal him now. There lie his bones, protected by the Heart of the Saviour.' It seemed such an odd thing to write, I can remember it very clearly. Perhaps it's a clue as well."

"Excellent," I said. "So we have a tomb above the First Cataract, on an island between the temples of Isis and Augustus, protected by the Heart of Christ, and revealed by the noon sun. That's a lot to go on, and I say we start at once."

* * *

A couple of hours later, we found ourselves in a felucca, another Nile boat but much smaller than a dahabiyah, plying out from the little marina south of the Aswan Dam, into a maze of craggy little islands protruding out of the still blue waters of the reservoir. Omar sat at the tiller, a couple of the Syrian crewmen sculled away, and I sat in the prow, flanked by Ari and Serpe; Maria was watching the children, back in Elephantine. To our starboard stretched the gleaming concrete of the dam, a thin line of white between the sapphire of the lake and the sapphire of the sky.

Plunging in among the islands, our prow turned left and right under the capable guidance of Omar.

I had brought the glass-bottomed bucket from the *Ghazal*, and now I lowered it into the waters and peered at the rocky bed of the lake, remarkably clear and close. Silver fish flitted into and out of my view. I passed the bucket to Ari.

"There it is—the Temple of Isis!" exclaimed Serpe, and we all looked forward.

It looked like a ship made of stone. A pair of colonnades stretched out towards us through the waters, like its gunwales; behind them rose tall blocks of masonry, which I assumed to be the temple itself, like the cabins in the stern of an oil tanker.

"Steer us close, Omar," I called back. "Let's find a way of climbing up to the top of those colonnades—I bet we can see for miles from there."

The felucca turned in towards the temple, and we slid between the colonnades. The colonnade on the right was a lot shorter than the other, so our view was unobstructed of another large temple, rising out of the waters beyond, all columns, with leafy designs around the capitals.

"Could that be the temple of Augustus?" I wondered.

Serpe looked at it a long while. "It is not Egyptian," he admitted. "It *looks* Roman."

"It *looks* like a wedding cake," I remarked. I reached for the brown leather case of my binoculars and, unbuckling it, raised them to my eyes. The temple was open to the sky—perhaps it had had a wooden roof in the past. It slid out of sight behind the colonnade, and I lowered the binoculars. "We should check that place out," I commented.

The colonnade to our right had been at one time a covered walk, now without a roof, the upper halves of broken columns projecting like fangs from the waters. On the opposite side, the colonnade was more elaborate, the upper parts of doorways showing at regular intervals.

But ahead of them stood the massive double towers of the temple, or as Ari called them, the propylons. As the felucca advanced along the colonnade, they dwarfed us, grim guardians of the sanctuary of the Egyptian goddess.

We could see now, carved deeply into the walls, the figures of people in the Egyptian style. On the left, a man, twelve or fourteen feet high, was holding a number of much smaller people by the hair and brandishing a long club at them. On the right was the image of a woman.

"Why does she have a football on her head?" I asked.

"That's Isis," Ari replied, "the mother of the pharaohs, and that's not a soccer ball, as you know very well—it's a sun-disc between the horns of a cow."

"How could I have been so silly!" I remarked. "Aren't all the fashionable Egyptian goddesses wearing them?"

Three doorways, much shortened by the height of the water, stood before us, and we took the middle one into a quadrangle with further propylons before us. To our right was what looked like some kind of pagan chapel, fronted with columns with a strange face at the top of each.

Seeing my puzzlement, Ari said, "That must be a chapel to Hathor. Those faces are her—she had some cow-features."

I nodded. "The Egyptians are strange." Turning in the other direction, I saw that illustrated on the colonnade opposite were various figures that combined human and animal features—a woman with a hippopotamus body, a fat human body with a crocodile head, and so forth. I felt a creeping sensation descend along my spine and touched the rosary in my breast pocket.

The sun went out as we passed through another doorway into another roofless colonnaded area, but this one was still painted in colours that transformed the columns into a forest of lime greens, turquoise blues and coral pinks, vivid as they had been thousands of years ago, though beginning to flake now.

Ari pointed. About a foot above the water, someone had carved a cross into each of the columns. They looked a little like the Maltese crosses I had seen on the wings of German and Austrian aeroplanes during the war.

"Coptic Christians," Ari said. "This place was used as a church."

"It must have been a very creepy Christian church," I observed softly.

The Syrians rowing shipped their oars, and the boat slowed, bumping gently against the further wall. Omar pulled on the tiller, and we came to rest where well-worn steps led out of the water.

In the shadows under the portico, the brightness of Omar's eyes revealed his apprehension.

"Effendi," he said, "here you may climb to the roof of this place. I warn you—have a care."

"Will you come with us, Omar?" I asked.

But the dragoman shook his head. "This place is thick with something your servant's poor brain cannot reckon. I shall stay with the boat and await your return, effendim."

Ari, Serpe and I climbed the steps, emerging into the blistering air within a short while. The roof was an uneven place, pock-marked, sometimes with collapsed masonry leaving gaping holes, sometimes square-cut apertures leading by means of steps into chambers below. I shone my torch into a few of these, and caught sight of wall images depicting mummification or a woman with wings like a hawk.

"What a view!" exclaimed Ari.

Across the water from us, to the south, we saw another set of ruins on the far side of fifty yards of water: just a couple of broken columns and, beyond them, a pair of archways.

"I think it has writing on it," Ari said, pointing.

I took out my binoculars and trained them on the ruins. "It's in Latin," I said. Serpe took the binoculars from me and after a few seconds of mouthing the words silently, read aloud: "*AVGVSTVS DEO IMPERATORQUE HIC COLEBAT.*" And Ari translated for me: "Augustus, god and emperor, is worshipped here."

Chapter 5
The Crypt

We reached the temple of Augustus about twenty minutes later. The mood on the felucca was electrified; even Omar caught it, singing softly to himself as he brought the boat in a wide arc close to the Roman ruins.

"Let's see what we can find down below." I looked again through the glass-bottomed bucket. I could see paving stones below. There had been something like a pavement there, centuries ago. "Can we row slowly in circles?" I asked. Omar nodded, and we started to move in circles, each one getting tighter as we rowed towards the middle.

"What do you see, Macaroni?" asked Serpe, staring into the waters beside me.

"Well, the pavement down there is not even," I explained. "Some parts of it are raised."

"Earthquake?"

"No—too regular."

"Perhaps the remains of old walls?" suggested Serpe.

"I don't think so," I said, "but it's hard to see. I think I'll have to go down there."

I stripped down to my shorts and climbed over the side. The water was deliciously cool, and I found

I could not quite touch the bottom and still keep my head face above the water. I kicked away from the boat and dived under. I could see everything down there, fading to a blue-grey distance. But I hadn't much breath, and had to keep returning to the surface.

Then I found what I was looking for.

The raised portions of the pavement stood about four inches high, and were about the same in width. They extended in a wide sweep in many directions, but there didn't seem to be any pattern to them, at least not from my perspective, though they seemed to be very deliberate. And although they were the same colour as the pavement upon which they were built, the colour was just slightly different, as if they had been exposed to less sun and weather than the pavement.

I returned to the surface.

"What did you find?" asked Ari.

I explained my discovery. "Those little walls were put there on top of an existing pavement, and at a much later date."

Ari looked up at the sun. "The afternoon is wasting," she observed. "The noon sun isn't going to reveal anything to us now."

I sighed. "Perhaps you're right." I hauled myself into the felucca, Ari's hands helping me along.

"The afternoon is a-wasting," repeated Serpe quietly. "'Only the sun of noon can reveal him now.'" He looked up at the sun for a moment, squinting and shielding his eyes. "*Che ora sono?*"

I consulted my pocket-watch. "Two-thirty." I was sitting in a puddle in the boat, toweling myself down. "Perhaps these walls have nothing to do with Bohemund's tomb."

Serpe scratched the top of his head thoughtfully. "At noon, how would those walls be different from any other time? How is it that the sun of noon could reveal them?"

"Perhaps the sun would cast shadows that would reveal the entrance to Bohemund's tomb," suggested Ari.

"But at noon," said Serpe, "there are no shadows—the sun is almost directly over our heads."

Ari gave a gasp. We all turned to her. "Is it *noon*, or *none*?" I couldn't hear any difference, the way she said it. We stared blankly at her, and she hurried to explain: "In the Middle Ages, they didn't usually measure the day in twenty-four hours. The passage of time was marked by the canonical hours, the hours at which religious houses prayed. The fourth hour, three o'clock in the afternoon, was called *none* or *nones*. N-O-N-E, not N-O-O-N."

I leaped to my feet, so vigorously that we shipped a little water. "What are we waiting for? We have half an hour! We need to be in a high place."

Omar called out to the oarsmen and we turned about, sliding smoothly through the waters back to the Temple of Isis. A few minutes later, all of us except the crewmembers were scrambling up some stone steps to the topmost tower of the temple. We emerged into daylight, and from there commanded a fair view of the lake, the islands, and particularly the flat stretch of water between the temples of Isis and Augustus. I could see vaguely the indistinct shapes of the raised portions of the pavement through the clear waters. The sun was declining towards the west, but still high in the sky at this hour, of course; and as it moved, the shadows sharpened and new shadows came into focus.

And suddenly, at the canonical hour of nones, three in the afternoon, the shadows coalesced, and dark lines appeared beneath the still waters.

First came the outline of a face, then the shoulders and a hand raised in benediction.

Slowly, eyes appeared.

A long, straight nose came next, then a beard.

The other hand emerged, its forefinger extended towards something we couldn't see yet.

Three o'clock precisely arrived. Very distantly, from the shore, a muezzin summoned the faithful to afternoon prayer. And down in the courtyard below, a shape like a heart appeared.

It was a depiction of Christ, and the tip of His extended forefinger pointed to His Sacred Heart.

Ari quoted from Bohemund's manuscript: "'And there lie his bones now, protected by the heart of the Saviour.'"

If we were reading the clues right, we had found the Tomb of Bohemund.

We hurried back down the steps and into the felucca, where Serpe gave directions to Omar. Moments later, I had torn off my shoes and slipped over the side, out of the arid Egyptian heat and into the cool waters.

"I'll be with you in a moment," said Ari, as I clung onto the gunwale.

"Did you bring a bathing suit?" I asked.

Ari plucked at her shirt. "It's underneath this. I won't be long."

Taking a deep breath, I plunged beneath the water. Moments later, Ari joined me, and together we dived and explored, then came up for air, and then went down again. It seemed to take for ever, as we had no way of breathing underwater—we had left our suits on the LS3, which, of course, was currently in Germany.

After more dives than I could count, we finally located the Heart. It consisted of raised bricks enclosing a space about four feet wide. I ran my fingers along the inside and then the outside of the brick rim, but located no mechanism. Then I turned my attention to the space inside the rim.

Ari joined me, her hair wafting about her head in a dark cloud. Together, we found that the medieval bricklayer had arranged the bricks in a perfect circle, about a yard across. He had formed the image of a Cross in the middle of the circle, like the crosses we had seen in the Temple of Isis.

Something about that precise arrangement of cross and circle reminded me of something very familiar, but I couldn't place it.

But Ari and I both needed air, and we returned to the surface.

On the next dive, I tried moving the brick circle with a knife, while Ari cleared away the weeds that might impede its movement. But it didn't budge. I wasted another two dives trying to loosen it by running the point of my knife all the way around the perimeter of the circle, but to no avail. We hadn't moved it even a fraction of an inch.

"It looks so familiar to me," I said during a brief respite, while we clung to the side of felucca. "It's as if I've seen it a thousand times."

"What is there you've seen a thousand times?" Ari asked.

"Well, there's your face," I replied. "Apart from that, I can't think of anything."

Serpe, leaning over the side of the boat, asked, "What about the insignia on German aircraft during the war?"

"That can't be the answer," I said.

"What about that book you're always reading?" asked Ari. "You know, Brown's *Mechanical Movements*?"

"Of course!" I was so surprised, I almost leaped out of the water. "Number 371—the modification of the mangle-wheel motion!"

"The what?"

"Ah, Number 371!" exclaimed Serpe, recalling our days at Imperial.

"The large wheel," I explained, "is toothed on both faces, and an alternating circular motion is produced by the uniform revolution of the pinion, which passes from one side of the wheel to the other through an opening in the circumference of the wheel."

"How silly of me," said Ari. "How could I have missed that?" Under her breath, she added, "*Now* who's talking like a professor?"

I reached forward and kissed her. "At least, that disc must have a pinion and, since it's not visible to us, it must be on the underside. That means there's a way of turning the pinion, probably a circular hole in the side of the wheel. If we had a pair of pliers, I cold probably turn it."

Serpe threw open the lid of the box he had brought with him and handed me his pliers. I put them in the waterproof belt-pouch I always wore on such occasions then, grinning, Ari and I went down together once more.

I felt around the outside of the wheel, until I discovered a small hole, out of which protruded the small stem that, if I was right, turned a pinion. It took a couple of separate dives, since it was stiff with age. But then I hit upon the idea of taking the bucket down with me. By keeping it inverted, I was able to keep a bucketful of air, and I found I could work a little longer by breathing from the bucket during my dives.

Slowly, the stem turned, and to my wonder, the wheel started turning too. It continued to be stiff—after all, the mechanism was five hundred years old—but in the end, I had completed a revolution.

Suddenly, two things happened at once. The first was that the pinion reached the opening, which was invisible to us, in the circumference of the wheel, and the pressure on the other side caused it to flip upwards. The second was that a huge bubble of air broke from the opening left by the wheel, wobbling and ascending right between me and Ari. The air below having disappeared, the water surged down what was now a hole, and the suction caught my feet and dragged me through it.

All was dark, cold chaos for a few moments. The water dragged me down a chute, smacking me over and over against close stone walls. I wanted to scream, but there was no air. I wanted to stop myself, but the motion was too great.

Suddenly, the chute through which I had descended widened out. I floundered for a moment, disoriented. Sometimes, it's difficult to tell which way is up underwater, especially when there's no light. I tried to relax, and felt my body slowly start to rotate. I struck something else, something soft. I didn't know what it was.

A moment later, my face broke the surface of the water, and I hungrily sucked air into my lungs. I threw up a quick prayer of thanks—I hadn't had time to ask for help on the descent.

I was in a darkness more total than anything I'd ever experienced before. Shutting my eyes would have made no difference to it at all.

But I could hear. Someone or something was splashing nearby and gasping for air. "Ari?" I gulped.

"Here, Mac."

She must have been sucked down the chute with me, and she had been the soft thing I had knocked against a few moments ago.

I reached out and tried to explore what was around me. My fingertips found something hard and slippery, and I pulled myself towards it. It was solid and uneven—rock. I spent a few moments catching my breath, then said, "Where are we?"

"I don't know," came Ari's voice. "Have you found dry land?"

"I've found wet land," I answered. "Nothing here is dry."

Water slapped against my shoulders as Ari found the rock beside me. I heard her fingers scrabbling against the rock. "It's only about three feet above the water," she said, and I heard a rush of water as she pulled herself up; I followed her, and a moment later we sat together on a rock shelf, still in complete darkness.

Opening the canvas pack on my belt, I took out my electric torch and switched it on. Ari looked pale and cold in the faint light. I put my arm around her and held her tight. I could feel her shivering, and her hair was cold as she put her head on my shoulder.

"Where are we?" she asked, her teeth chattering as she spoke.

I shone the torch around. "We came out of what looks like a circular basin, full of water. We're on a shelf of rock. The roof's just a few feet over our heads." I turned my head and shone the torchlight behind us. "That's interesting. There's a hole in the rock right behind us. Just a moment—I'll see what it is."

I crawled on all fours towards this new opening and shone the torch through it. It illuminated a sandy floor below.

"Well, that way's dry, at least."

Ari joined me and peered through the opening.

"You see what happened?" I said. "We fell down that long chute, which had a curve at the bottom of it, and ended up here. It's like a valve, like one you'd use for winemaking, or an airlock. Somebody wanted to keep things down here very dry."

"Bohemund, do you think?"

"Perhaps."

"Well," said Ari, "we won't find out sitting here."

I felt it my duty to point out another course of action. "It's only right to say that we can actually get out the way we came."

Ari nodded, and I noticed that not only was she no longer shivering, but her eyes shone with excitement.

"All right," I said, holding up my hands in instant surrender, "let's see what we can find and then go back. Maybe Bohemund is close."

One by one, we wriggled through the opening and dropped perhaps ten or twelve feet to the sandy floor of a room below.

I had pocketed the torch so we could climb through the opening, and now I flipped the switch again.

A grey face stared at us from only a few feet away, and we both let out a yelp of terror.

Its eyes were empty sockets, the mouth gaped wide, with brown, uneven teeth, and the skin was stretched taut over high cheekbones. A tuft of grey hair clung to the domed skull. Whoever the face belonged to was lying on his side.

Neither of us moved for a long time, though the circle of electric light trembled a little.

Ari took a deep breath. "Nothing to fear from the dead," she said and, making the Sign of the Cross, advanced past me towards the skeleton. It was laid out on an old wooden shelf, about five feet from the ground. It had been lying on its back, but over the long years, the head had slipped to the side. I ran the torch-beam the length of the body. Ribs poked through dusty rags, and the hands folded upon the chest were bleached bones. I moved the torch-beam around, and saw that other horrid figures like this one lined the walls all about. This had been a place to lay to rest the dead, and there were many, many of them in this crypt. The bodies were shelved three high all about, like books in a grisly library, some wrapped in winding sheets or bandages, others more loosely shrouded. There was nothing else in the room.

"Well," I said, and my voice seemed to tremble, "this is a pleasant little spot we've discovered."

Opposite the place where we had entered, we could see a dark doorway, framed roughly in stone. Shining the light down it, we saw that exiting the crypt would take us along a downwards-sloping tunnel about six feet wide and maybe seven feet high.

“The ancient Egyptians made very fine tunnels,” observed Ari, “and the First Cataract was a place where they built temples and homes for the wealthy. The tunnels made it easy for the rich people to get quickly to the temples.”

At that moment, a frightful wail echoed about the vault, and Ari and I leaped into each other’s arms. I dropped the torch, and the light went out.

Chapter 6
The Tomb of Bohemund

The hairs on the back of my scalp rose. My mouth was dry. The wail had seemed like a howl of deep despair, of a creature without hope.

The wail came again, but this time it was intelligible: "Ma-ca-*ron*-i!"

I gave a gasp. "Serpe?"

"Where are you?" It was Serpe's voice all right, but he was still in the airlock, which is what had made it echo.

I felt around on the floor, located the torch, and switched it on, dashing for the opening. Moments later, Serpe dropped to the floor beside us. I almost laughed—he wore an old-fashioned bathing suit that covered everything to his knees and elbows. It was striped in red, green and white, like an Italian flag. Like me, he wore a utility belt with a couple of waterproof pouches.

"Why you laugh, Macaroni?" he asked.

I shook my head. "Never mind," I said. "I'm very glad to see you."

"What is here?" Taking his own torch out of one of his pouches, Serpe stepped out into the centre of the crypt and turned about, his eyes wide.

"We found a crypt," Ari told him.

Serpe gave a slow nod. "Is Bohemundo here?" he asked.

"We haven't searched yet," Ari replied.

It amazed me, when I thought about it, how much braver we felt now there were three of us. We began to examine the bodies methodically, one after another. There were very few possessions with them, nothing to give away their identities.

"These bodies," Serpe explained, "did not belong to *Egiziani.* The *Egiziani,* they placed things belonging to the dead person with him."

"Grave goods," added Ari. "Things they'd need in the afterlife."

"What would you need in the afterlife?" I wondered.

"To the Egyptians, the afterlife was exactly like this one, but unending. So they needed the same kinds of things they'd owned in life." She glanced at the bodies in the crypt. "The lack of grave goods suggests that these are Christian burials."

"I found a crucifix with one," I said.

Ari nodded. "But that's more like an article of clothing than grave goods." A shiver ran through her body. "I'm getting cold. Shall we move on?"

However hot Egypt was, it was cold down here, and we all wore damp clothes. We moved off along the passageway, led by the dim yellow pool of Serpe's torch. The passage wound left and right until we couldn't tell which way we were walking.

Serpe called a pause for a moment, while he changed the batteries in his torch. Ari's fingers entwined about mine and squeezed gently while we waited in total darkness. Of course, I had my own torch, but it didn't seem necessary to waste energy.

Serpe gave a curse in Italian and something—one of the batteries, I guessed—hit the floor. It bounced. There was silence for a few seconds, and then we heard it strike the ground again, but far off.

Serpe and Ari gasped.

I flicked on my torch and shone it at the floor in front of Serpe.

We were less than a foot from the edge of a great gaping chasm, the whole width of the passageway, so deep we could not see its floor.

Ari gave a gulp. "One more step . . . " She crossed herself.

I aimed the beam of my torch down the pit. The pale shapes of someone's bones gleamed from the bottom of the chasm. His arm was extended, and between his fingers something glinted. It was the battery Serpe had dropped.

"It looks like he caught it," I observed.

"Poor soul," remarked Ari, and we prayed for him.

The pit wasn't difficult to leap over, and in a few minutes we were underway again, keeping the light trained on the floor now.

Before long, we came across a room, dug out of the rock to the right of the passageway. It contained more ancient dead, grinning at us from the shadows. We all stepped cautiously inside, Serpe letting the torchlight roam quickly about this new chamber.

"What's that?" The torchlight outlined Ari's slender arm and shoulder as she pointed at something near the ceiling. Serpe focused the torch where she pointed, and now we all saw a gleam of metal, perhaps gold. It came from the very top shelf, and I had to put my foot onto the lower shelf, feeling it shift slightly, to reach it.

"Be careful," warned Ari.

"Aren't I always?" On the top shelf, my torch revealed the remains of a man, his skull, ribs and fingers darkened with age, robed in what had been white linen but was now dirty rags. His hands, folded upon his chest, enclosed a clay box, covered with etched hieroglyphics.

"This is Egyptian," I said over my shoulder, and described what I could see. "The lid seems to resemble a scarab beetle, and there's a band of gold beneath it that goes all the way around it."

I pulled gently on the box, but it wouldn't move. "Come on, old boy," I said, "you don't need this any more."

"Leave it," said Ari. "It's not important."

"How do you know that?" Leaning a little closer, I lifted the scarab-lid about half an inch and looked inside.

There was nothing in it, and I let the lid drop. I was about to climb down when something from underneath it made the lid pop up. I cried out in surprise, and again the shelf under my feet shifted.

A pair of clubbed antennae pushed out from under the lid, followed by the horned head of a scarab beetle. The lid dropped behind it, but then it stirred and another beetle emerged, and another, and another. They started swarming over the shelf and towards the floor.

I jumped back down to the floor. Ari, seeing the beetles for the first time, stiffened and grabbed my arm.

"They're just harmless little scarab beetles," I said, though my flesh crawled to see them, to hear their feet rattling against the shelves as more and more of them erupted from the box on the top shelf.

"It doesn't matter," answered Ari. "I just . . . don't . . . like them." She started backing away; they were all over the floor by now.

"Where are they all coming from?" I wondered, backing away beside Ari.

"*A chi importa?*" exploded Serpe. "I do not know, but also, I do not care—*I* leave now!" Serpe beat a hasty retreat from the scarab chamber, Ari and me with him.

But Serpe had come to a halt outside, and was running the torch-beam around the walls and floor of the passageway.

"What is it?" asked Ari, a slight tremor in her voice.

"One more hole," said Serpe, and the torchlight illuminated its edge and the sharp points of six-foot spikes thrusting up towards the unsuspecting explorer.

Then something else caught my eye. "Why is the floor moving?" I asked.

Serpe turned the torch behind us, and we all three screamed. The floor was a seething mass of scarab beetles.

"They're harmless. They're harmless. They're harmless," muttered Ari.

My flesh crawling, my gorge rising, I turned. Behind us was an army of scarab beetles, ahead of us an impassable pit full of lethal spikes.

Well, God, I prayed, this is the life you've given me.

Steeling myself, I turned back to the insects and leaped in among them. I could feel their tough carapaces, their horny antennae sharp against my bare feet. With a terrible tickling, they scrambled over the tops of my toes. Dashing back into the chamber, I flicked on my torch with a trembling thumb.

The shelf I had stood on had shifted under my weight, I recalled, so it must be loose.

Reaching down, I took hold of the bottom shelf and tugged. It was loose, all right, but not free. More scarab beetles dropped from above, skittering over my hands. I flinched and caught my breath. The wretched little beasts were all over the shelf I was attempting to extract, all over the wood and all over the skeleton upon it. I couldn't touch it without touching *them.*

Forcing myself not to think about it, I pushed down on one end of the shelf and tried to wiggle it loose.

I felt something light drop onto my head. It moved through my hair and down my shirt. I tensed all over. More than anything, I wanted to run. I didn't care if there were spikes in the pit, I just wanted the beetles gone.

They were all over my shoulders now, and crawling down my shirt, on the inside and the outside.

Shouting with a horror I couldn't explain, I ripped off my shirt and shook it violently. I heard several spatters as beetles hit the walls.

I rolled up my shirt and stuffed it into my belt. Then I reached down once again to the shelf, batting aside scarabs, or letting them pelt me from above.

My only way out, I thought. My only way out.

I pried upwards on the shelf. The bones on top of it rattled as they slid backwards—something that would probably have horrified me half an hour ago. I hauled on the shelf, and at last it came loose in my hands. Tucking it under my arm, I ran out and joined Ari and Serpe, right on the edge of the pit. I set the shelf down on the near edge, then slowly lowered the other end; it was just long enough to reach.

"Off you go," I said.

Making the Sign of the Cross, Serpe went first. The shelf bounced under him, and he had to slow down. All the time, beetles rattled out onto the shelf on their nasty little feet. They ran over my hands, too, for I was holding down the near end.

A piece of wood came off in my hand, and I held it close to my eye as Ari shone light on it. It was rotten.

"I have crossed!" called Serpe.

"I don't know that this plank is safe," I said quietly.

Ari took a look at the spikes in the pit and the scarab beetles swarming out of the dark crypt. "Are you kidding?" she said and, thrusting the torch into my hand, took off along the narrow little bridge. She was across in a moment, and it was my turn.

Putting my foot out, I tested my weight on the ancient wood.

It's not going to hold, I suddenly understood, especially if I go slowly, feeling my way. But it would be weakest in the middle, relatively stable at either end.

Then there's only one way to do it, I concluded.

"Here, catch this, and light my way!" I tossed the torch to Ari, who caught it. She and Serpe each turned a narrow beam onto the narrow strip of wood, swarming with the horrid little creatures, that lay between me and the deathly spikes.

Consigning myself to divine protection, I put one foot ahead of me onto the plank, then went into a low crouch. A moment later, I sprang, flying out over the abyss. My outstretched foot touched the middle of the bridge, and I pushed down with it. I flew forward. Behind me, the plank slid off the side of the chasm. But I sailed forward, reaching out for the further edge of the pit. I hit it with a blow that drove all the air out of my lungs. I felt a sharp point press into the ball of my foot.

But just as I started to slip, I felt hands grasp my upper arms, and Ari and Serpe hauled me to safety. In a moment, the three of us were sprawled on the floor on the far side of the pit. Serpe leaped to his feet and started thrashing at the beetles that had gained our side, until they were all dead.

"But they can climb," he said, panting. "*Andiamo.*"

The passage curved round and up, and after twenty feet or so, emerged into a circular vault, with shelves along the edges, like the others, and a large sarcophagus in the middle. We looked around at the dead on the shelves, then at each other.

All together, we moved towards the sarcophagus. On top of it was an image of Christ, like the one we had seen in the lake, and around the edge were etched into the stone words in a Roman script: HIC JACET IN CVSTODELA CORDIS CHRISTI BOEMVNDVS SERVVS REGIS SERSVRAE. ORATE PRO EO.

A smile growing across her lips, Ari translated: "Here, under the protection of the Heart of Christ, lies Bohemund, Servant of the King of Zerzura. Pray for him."

So we did pray for him. For at last, we had found Bohemund of Zerzura.

"So there he is!" breathed Ari in an awed whisper. With an almost reverential caress, she put her fingertips on the tomb's lid and walked about it, studying it from a variety of angles.

Serpe and I looked at each other. We knew what was going to happen next. Each of us took a position at either end of the sarcophagus, hooked our fingertips under the lid, and fixed the other with his eyes.

"On three," I said. "One, two, three!"

I could feel the veins standing out in my arms and pulsing in my temples. Serpe grew red in the face. Ari pushed, her face quivering with effort. Her feet slid on the sandy floor.

The lid made a scraping noise. It moved about an inch.

We all flopped onto the ground, panting and wringing our hands.

"Are you all right?" I asked.

"I've grazed the heel of my hand," replied Ari. "It's all right—nothing bad. It just stings a little, that's all. And I wish I had something to drink—I didn't expect to be down here so long."

"Yes, I'm thirsty too," I said quietly. I pulled myself to my feet. "Shall we try again?

We all got to our feet, our faces grim and determined in the faded light of the torches. We put our shoulders under the rim. On Ari's count, we heaved.

The lid scraped along the top edge, and a musty smell flowed out of the growing gap.

All at once, it slid off. Striking the floor, the stone lid broke in half, a jagged line right through the middle. Serpe stooped over double, bracing his arms against his knees. I wiped sweat from my brow. Ari was breathing noisily.

Slowly, amazed, we turned to the tomb of Bohemund.

"Mac—look at this!" Ari reached into the tomb and took out a bright golden object which she handed to me. Beginning to grin, I passed it in wonder to Serpe.

"The three-lobed key," he remarked with a smile.

"The Key of Zerzura!" Ari added, taking it back from him. "What else does he have, I wonder?"

I bent over the coffin myself. Bohemund had been arrayed in his finery. He wore a tall headpiece, like the crown of the pharaohs, inlaid with gold. Now it had slid to the side and rested against the wall of the coffin. At his side lay a sword, the scabbard turned long ago into dust, except the gold clasps. Around his shoulders was a cloak, which sparkled when Ari shone the torch on it: thread of gold had been spun into some long-decayed fabric. But the gold remained, an echo of splendour.

"Aha! What is this?" wondered Serpe. The Key had been concealing a small wooden box, about six inches square and three deep, with gold corners and an inlaid top.

I reached in and lifted the box from Bohemund's sunken chest. It was not locked, but the lid fit very snugly, and it was with some effort that I pried it off. When it did come off, it did it with a quiet pop and a sigh, almost like relief. Within it I found a neatly-folded piece of parchment, which I handed to Ari. It had not rotted, like everything else in the sarcophagus—presumably, the box had preserved it. With infinite care, Ari unfolded it and held it out for us all to see.

The corner of her mouth twitched up in a smile. "I love maps!" she said.

"That looks like Egypt, and the Nile, and that's the coastline as far as Tripoli," I said, pointing to each of the features in turn. It was obviously a medieval map, and the land-masses didn't look quite as they would on a modern map; but features were still recognizable.

"And that," Serpe said, placing the tip of his forefinger on the map towards the middle bottom, "is Zerzura."

We all leaned in close and pored over the detail Serpe had indicated. Mountains stretched in a shallow V-shape with a mouth that pointed east; at the point was an ink drawing of a tower, shaded in a brown that had once been white. Surrounded by a cluster of well-drawn palm-trees, it was labeled VRBIS SERSVRAE.

"Well, it doesn't get any easier than that, does it?" I said in wonder. Secretly, I thought, What a boring adventure—just too easy.

Little did I know that the next twenty-four hours would prove me wrong on both counts.

Chapter 7
Back Into the Light

In the meantime, we still had to get back to the surface. Obviously, going back over the pits and wading through scarab beetles wasn't a good idea, if there was any other way. So we set about searching for another exit. We must have been searching for almost twenty minutes, when I noticed that the light from my torch was flickering.

"Do you have any more batteries?" I asked Serpe.

He shook his head and went back to his search. His torch wasn't much stronger than mine.

"Mac, Cristofero—come here." Ari had found something—she had felt air blowing across her feet from the foot of the wall and, stooping down and shining the light on it, I found there to be a narrow gap at the base of the wall.

"And this is wood, not stone," I declared, running my hand over it. Smiling, I added: "Yes, I thought so—a catch!"

I flipped the catch and pushed on the door. It moved with a slight reluctance, as if the hinges were rusty, and it groaned. It stopped when it was open about four inches. Dirt and debris had piled up behind it. Shining my torch through the gap, I saw that the wreckage, which had once been the ceiling, had entirely blocked the passage on the other side of the door.

"How will we move this?" wondered Serpe.

A light went off in my mind, and I reached into my waterproof pouch.

"What is this?" Serpe frowned, moving in close.

"This, my friend, is orichalcum, or Fire Stone. It's been in our family for years. Give me your torch."

I unscrewed the end of Serpe's torch. "Stand back," I said, and we all retired to the far end of the chamber. Ari crouched behind the tomb of Bohemund, and pulled Serpe down beside her. I positioned the orichalcum carefully then, with some trepidation, pressed the exposed end of the battery to it.

Immediately, with a deafening crash a blinding light lit up all the reposing bodies for an eerie second. I dropped behind the sarcophagus just as bits of stone and wood came flying over our heads, pelting the walls of the chamber. For a moment, we could see nothing, blinded by the flash. The air smelt of ozone.

Then Serpe started laughing.

"*Viva* the engineers!" he cried in delight. We all rose and looked with him towards the doorway.

The orichalcum had blasted a hole right through the fallen debris, revealing a short passage leading to

the bottom steps of a spiral staircase that wound rapidly out of sight.

I hastily reassembled Serpe's torch and we began ascending the spiral steps. They seemed to go on and on through complete darkness, getting more complete as the torch finally failed. Before long our breath was rasping and our feet were heavy as we laboured upwards. But then, I noticed that the air had begun to grow warmer, and a blue light seemed to have grown around us. The air smelled sweeter, and I wondered where on earth the passage would exit.

I did not have to wait long. Turning about the central column of the stairs one last time, we came upon a small window with three iron bars; beyond it, moonlight shimmered on deep blue waters.

Serpe and I took out our knives, and made short work of the ancient concrete around the iron bars. One by one, we squeezed through the gap and into the cool waters beyond.

We had emerged into the temple of Isis, and judging from the shade of the sky, about an hour after sunset. We swam to the staircase by which we had ascended earlier that day, and at last threw ourselves down, dripping, on the flat roof. I was the first to start laughing; then Ari joined in, and finally Serpe. For a few minutes, we were helpless with mirth. Then Serpe said, "Why do we laugh?"

"I don't know," I said. "That's adventures for you. But, well, scarab beetles—they're perfectly harmless."

"That didn't matter down there," Ari answered. She was staring up at the dazzling panoply of stars above us. "We were never in danger," she said quietly, "never once, for a moment. We were all safe in His hands." Her finger pointed up to the heavens. "It's funny we thought we were in danger."

"El Cracken!" came a voice I hadn't heard for several lifetimes. I jumped to my feet and looked over the edge of the roof. Below us floated the felucca. In the moonlight, I could see Omar's bearded face turned up towards me.

"Effendim!" he cried. "I hear the laughter, and I know it must be my master, El Cracken!"

I can't say that there wasn't a lot of celebrating that night on board the *Ghazal*, and that it didn't include the serious imbibing of whisky, champagne cocktails and grappa, and the smoking of cigars. Over a sumptuous dinner, prepared with haste by Omar, we planned the following day: we would rent camels and ride off into the desert in search of Zerzura. Omar remained aloof and silent during this conversation, but smiled winningly when he was addressed and answered with dignified respect when asked a question regarding the desert.

"Could Assumpta follow us to Zerzura, do you think?" Ari asked Omar at one point.

"Honoured lady, not likely at all," he said. "The signs remain for a long time in the desert, and one who can read them may follow in another's tracks, even years afterwards, but only when they have spent many years learning how."

"Do you know how, Omar?"

Omar bowed his head gravely. "It is many years since I have lived in the desert, honoured lady, but one does not forget."

Rose burped and her head fell backwards gently into the crook of Ari's arm. She began to snore softly. "You know," said Ari, "we've been thinking about renting camels, but what about Mr. Dawkins?"

"Is he for rent?" I was at the stage at which I had not quite had enough whisky.

"Don't be silly," returned Ari. "But you remember that Mr. Dawkins used to drive trucks into the desert during the war. That might be a faster way of crossing the desert than camels."

I nodded. "It might," I said, "but I don't think time's really an issue."

But that changed the following morning, when we discovered that someone had broken into the artifact room, cracked the safe, and stolen the key and the map.

* * *

"This dame is clever—very, very clever." Chesterton Valparaiso said. We had called him as soon as we had found out about the theft.

I looked at the mess of broken glass scattered all over the floor of the artifact room. "You think it's clever to leave all these clues around?"

Valparaiso looked me square in the eye. One of his eyes seemed to look over my shoulder.

Was it made of glass? I wondered.

"What do you think this dame is," Valparaiso demanded, "a housekeeper? No—the house she keeps is crime, her duster is a knuckle-duster, her mop is the mop of lawbreaking. She didn't need to cover her tracks up—she knew you'd know who was robbing you."

"She knew?"

"That's what I said."

"I know."

"I know too."

"What?"

"What you know—I know she knew it."

"I see."

"But do you? Do you really see the extent of this crime? Or are you trying to cover it up?"

"I don't think so."

"You don't think so—but what do you *know*, Mr. McCracken?"

"About what?"

"About this dame, this Bevan dame. You covered for her once before. Maybe you'd do it again."

I was beginning to feel bewildered. "I'm not covering for her now."

"Maybe, maybe not."

Fr. Murphy cleared his throat. "And what, may I ask, have you learned, Mr. Valparaiso?" he asked.

"Everything, Padre—everything. This room is crawling with clues, like a box full of spiders." He dropped his cigarette-butt to the floor and ground it out with his shoe. "She's probably halfway to freedom by now." Turning, he jabbed a stubby forefinger at Fr. Murphy. "Tell me, Padre, what do you know about this monk who went missing about the same time as the Bevan dame."

"Brother Osvaldo?" retorted Fr. Murphy, taken aback. "Why, nobody knew anything about him, except that it seems he isn't a brother at all."

"You say that," said Valparaiso, "but in the family of crime, he's the oldest brother, the heir to larceny. So here's what happens. The Bevan dame meets this Osvaldo, and they figure they have a common interest. They steal the goods—the dame had the know-how on how to break in and get away. What does the monk have? What's his angle?"

"Perhaps he has nothing to do with it at all, Mr. Valparaiso," suggested Fr. Murphy. "Perhaps he's just irrelevant."

Valparaiso wagged his head, almost in sorrow. "Nothing is irrelevant, Padre!" he said. "You just have to know what you're looking for, see?"

At this point, Omar entered, back from an errand upon which I had sent him. He bowed to the company and announced, "Effendi, I have spoken with a number of merchants in the city, and have learned that Miss Fortescue—"

"Who?" demanded Valparaiso.

"Miss Bevan's pseudonym."

"I learned that Miss *Bevan,*" Omar went on carefully, "rented a pair of camels yesterday, and was seen heading west in the company of one of these honourable Jesuit brothers at about six of the clock this morning."

Valparaiso gave a wise nod. "See? Now everything is clear!"

"We should rent camels and follow them," I suggested.

But Omar cleared his throat. "Effendim," he said, "might I suggest—you could not possibly catch up with Miss Fortescue on camels."

"Then what should we do?"

"Might I suggest," repeated Omar, "Mr. Dawkins, the Australian? It was your honourable wife's suggestion yesterday evening." He inclined his head towards Ari.

"Of course!" I said. "With his lorries, we'll catch up with them in no time!"

Ari took Omar to buy provisions while I sought out Digger's workshop. It didn't take me long to locate it—it was the only one in Aswan at the time.

The workshop was a fascinating place, containing two Model-T Ford lorries, a sedan I couldn't identify, and a plethora of spare parts, including inexplicably the propeller of an aeroplane, labeled *Wotan.* Oil and petrol cans lined the walls, piles of tyres, and shelves full of tools. The place was heavy with the smell of oil and petrol.

"Digger?" I called.

A sound came from near the roof: "Mmmmmm?"

"Digger, is that you?" Moving towards the back of the workshop, I saw that a rickety ladder led to a loft, but I couldn't see anything in it. "Digger?"

"She'll be apples, Mom," came Digger's sleepy voice. "Up in half a sec."

"I'm not your Mum," I told him. "It's me, McCracken—you remember me?" A long pause ensued, followed by a snore that sounded like someone ripping a piece of leather in two. "Digger!"

"Mm? Yeah, what? Sorry, sir. Sergeant Dawkins, reporting for duty. Lieutenant? Where are you?"

A pale face appeared out of the darkness of the loft and stared at me through narrow slits.

"You ain't the lieutenant. Who are you?"

"I'm McCracken," I explained. "Remember, we met after Mass, then you came to dinner on our boat."

Another long pause, then the slits widened into eyes. "Oh, right, so you are." He squinted again. "What time is it?" he asked.

I consulted my watch. "A little after noon."

"Bonzer. Time for a drink." There came a rustling from the loft, and a hand appeared just below the face. "Do us a favour, mate. Reach into the ice box down there and grab me a coolie."

The ice-box in question turned out to be full of beers, so I handed one up to Digger, who knocked the cap off on the edge of the loft and swigged down half the amber fluid in a single gulp. He gave a great sigh of relief and a prodigious burp.

"That's better! Now, 'scuse me a moment while I splash my boots, then I'll be right down."

He joined me a few moments later, tossing the empty bottle into a bin as he approached. Reaching into the ice-box, he drew out another and popped the cap. He offered it to me, but I shook my head.

"Now," said Digger, "what can I do for you?"

I explained the situation. When I had finished, he didn't speak for a long time, and I began to fear he'd fallen asleep on his feet. But then the beer-bottle rose to his lips and he swallowed another large gulp, though less ambitious than the previous ones. He looked appraisingly at the half-full bottle for a few moments. "Gets rid of morning-mouth better than toothpaste," he commented. Then he looked at me. "So these blokes, they started out about six o'clock this morning on camels?" I nodded. He glanced out of the window. "That means they're about sixty miles away, across the Sand Sea, as they call it. Overtaking them should be no sweat. Now, this billabong, what did you call it?"

"Zerzura."

"Where is it? What can you remember from the map?"

"It's hard to say—the measurements aren't precise. But it looked as if it was in the southwestern corner of the Sand Sea, about halfway to Tripoli."

Digger made an expression that looked like a wince, but turned out just to be a burp. "That's back of Bourke all right—probably about eight hundred miles. It'd take us ten or fifteen days by truck, assuming we can't drive straight as the cockatoo flies, which we never can."

"Do you think we should rent a plane?"

Digger shook his head. "I'm not opposed to that," he said, "but they're difficult to come by, and when you're in a plane, you're so high you don't have Buckley's chance of seeing the kind of details you need to see if you're tracking camels. Besides, it'll cost big bikkies to rent a plane. You got a tracker?" I reminded him of Omar. "Well, I don't like those blokes from the desert—I fought against 'em during the war. Still, that's your business, not mine."

"Won't you come with us?"

Digger gave another wince. "I can't, mate. I can rent you the trucks and sell you the petrol, but I have to work, so I can earn enough quid to get back to Aussie."

"If there were another way of getting back to Australia," I countered, "would you come with us?"

"I guess it depends," he replied. "What's on you mind?"

"My friend will be here in a few weeks—maybe just a few days—and we co-own an airship. We could take you back to Australia on that."

"An airship—like those bloody big things the Huns used to fly in the war?" He gave a low whistle. "Never seen one of them. Can they reach the Land of Oz?"

I nodded. "A lot more reliable than silver shoes."

Grinning, Digger raised his beer-bottle in a toast, and we had a deal.

Chapter 8
Libyan Sands

We left Aswan early the next morning. Ari had decided she and the children would stay behind, and it was with deep regret that I left the three of them in Elephantine in the dark hours.

There were, in any case, only two seats in each of the lorries, so Digger and Omar were assigned to the lead lorry, Valparaiso and I to the one behind. The seats were a little cramped. If there had been doors on the trucks, our knees would have been eight inches above them, but Digger had removed them. He had also removed the bonnet, and I asked him why.

"The biggest danger to vehicles in the desert," he explained, "is an overheating engine. This way, we keep the engine nice and cool."

"But doesn't sand get into it?"

"A bit," he replied, "but that's less of a problem than overheating."

Petrol cans were strapped onto the running-boards on both sides, and the back was piled high with crates of food, blankets, water cans, and a toolbox. Each truck had a pair of spare tyres strapped to the passenger's side.

The engines thrummed in the darkness, the headlights picking out the sandy ground ahead of us. Omar joined the rest of us, having inspected the lorries and particularly the supplies. He wore a jerd, a rectangular piece of woolen cloth four feet wide and fourteen long, which he wrapped about his body toga-fashion.

"We must leave," he said. "The sun is rising."

Indeed, behind us, the distant mountains were fringed with light, which was slowly extinguishing the stars above them.

"Should we inflate the tyres a bit first?" I asked. They seemed to be almost flat.

"Nah," answered Digger, swinging himself into the driver's seat of the lead lorry. "Fully inflated tyres will just sink in soft sand, so you have to spread the weight out a bit. I've deflated them all to about fifteen pounds per square inch."

Omar started to climb into the lorry beside him, but Digger held up his hand. "Mind if I show El Cracken a few things about driving first, Omar? Should only take a couple of hours."

Making the salaam, Omar climbed down, then he and Valparaiso clambered into the rear lorry while I joined Digger.

The lorry began to move, slowly at first, but building up speed until we were making about fifteen miles per hour. Around us, the light grew, the sands stretching golden in all directions. This was the Great Sand Sea: sand dunes in all directions, with nothing but sand in between, an ocean of sand, one ridge of sand after another, boundless and bare, all the way to the horizon. The dunes stood across our way, like a series of walls, each three hundred feet high.

"Do we have to go round them?" I asked, feeling extremely discouraged.

Digger shook his head. "This is the first lesson," he replied. "Watch this."

He jostled with the clutch and pressed down on the accelerator. The needle of the speedometer crept up: twenty miles an hour, thirty, thirty-five. I gripped the side of the lorry, and without thinking pressed my foot forward, as if I had some kind of control. A wall of yellow stood before us, and the lorry tipped backwards, quite violently. My teeth were parted, and an ululating cry escaped from between them. I felt that at any moment we would tip over backwards. The Australian sniggered wildly, hunched over the wheel.

Quite suddenly, we were at the top of the sand dune, three hundred feet above the others. Digger cut the engine, and we slewed to a stop. Looking behind us, I could see our tyre-tracks were barely half an inch deep, but everything I knew about driving told me we should have buried ourselves in the dune. Perhaps, I thought, the sand wasn't quite as loose here as elsewhere. But reaching down, I scooped up some of it and let it run between my fingers. It was as smooth and loose as the contents of an hour-glass.

"Now, do you think you can do that?" Digger asked.

I looked back at the other lorry, three hundred feet below us and two hundred yards behind. "You just go that fast?" I asked. "How does it work?"

Digger shrugged. "I don't know—we just found out how to do it during the war. Works every time, once you get the hang of it."

I took a deep breath. "I'll give it a shot."

"Do you know the fastest way down the side of a sand dune?" asked Digger, as I descended from the cab. I shook my head. "Sit down and slide on your bum."

Willing now to take Digger's word, I sat down on the edge of the dune. The sand was not as hot as I had expected it to be—the sun was not yet at its zenith. Cautiously, I pushed myself away from the summit and started sliding on my backside, starting rivers of disturbed grains of sand gushing ahead of me down the slope.

Immediately, all around me came a deep, harmonious throbbing sound, a low, melancholy vibrating hoot that filled my ears until I came to a rest at the foot of the dune.

"Did you hear that?" I demanded of Omar and Valparaiso, who approached me from the lorry.

"Yeah, I heard it—what's the low-down?" wondered Valparaiso.

Smiling, Omar said, "El Cracken, you have discovered the Singing Sands! That is the way of the desert—it will speak to thee. Sometimes, the wind stirs the sand, and the desert will speak of the times when grass grew here, and men and beasts lived here."

"Uncanny." I shivered a little. It must be the air-gaps between the sand-grains resonating as they stirred, I thought. But a scientific explanation didn't make it any less spooky.

I climbed into the lorry, but on my first attempt up the dune, I went too slowly. The lorry stalled about a third of the way up the dune, then slid backwards. I cut the engine, but too late—the spinning wheels dug deep ruts into the sand, and I was stuck.

Digger hastened down from the top of the dune, and he and Omar unslung long metal planks from the side of the lorry. They laid them under the wheels, and after about fifteen minutes we were able to reverse the lorry over them and out of the hole.

But I got it right the second time, and before too long we were speeding along the crest of the sand dune, stopping from time to time so that Omar could spring from the lead lorry to examine the ground for a few moments. Assumpta and Osvaldo seemed to have kept to the top of this dune for quite a way, but left it when they saw a cleft in the ridge off to the west; and we followed them in that direction too.

The dunes and rocky ridges of the Great Sand Sea run roughly north to south, which makes traveling west difficult. In between the dunes and ridges were wide expanses of sand, like a mirror that the sun struck on purpose to blind us, it seemed. I soon learned to drive with the windscreen down, since the glare of the sun on the glass made it impossible to see forward.

We would often see mirages, though they didn't fool us—we never thought there really was water there. They would hover before us, staying right at half a mile away or less, and sometimes they would extend outwards on either side until they surrounded us. It seemed as if we drove across a sandy island in the middle of a vast, steaming ocean. The blue disc of the sky, punched through by the sun, arced over us, the yellow disc of the Sand Sea below us, and these walls of water on all sides. I began to think I knew what it must have been like to be an Israelite with Moses, crossing the Red Sea.

As he tracked them, Omar deduced more and more about Assumpta's party. She and Br. Osvaldo had hired a third party, whom Omar guessed to be a guide. They had three additional camels with them, presumably as beasts of burden. Sometimes—rarely—they left something physical behind, like a food tin or, on one occasion, a book in Italian. Its title was *Giovanni Hus, Il Veridico*, by Benito Mussolini.

"Romans," said Omar, almost as if he were spitting.

"Do you mean *Italians*?" I asked.

Omar gave a quiet smile. "My people do not change quickly," he explained. "We still remember how the Romans invaded." With a wide gesture, he took in all the sands as far as the eye could see. "There are many ruins from the Romans here. So these Italians, invading now, to us they are just more Romans."

"I'm sure this fellow would be pleased by that comparison," I said, holding up the book.

"Mussolini ben-Ito," read Omar from the cover. "Who is this Son of Ito?"

"A rising star in Italy," I explained. "A very ambitious man." I tossed the book back into the sand. "There's something for a future archaeologist to puzzle about," I concluded.

Omar scanned the ground and pointed. "They went that way," he said, "about three days ago."

"How can you tell they went that way?" I asked, examining the ground as if I expected to see a bootprint, like Sherlock Holmes would have done.

Omar grinned. "There is no other way, effendim. That ridge extends many miles to the north and south, and there is only one gap—there. They ate their midday meal here and, mark my words, we shall find their camp in the gap between those two peaks, there."

And we did. We still had some hours of daylight left, so we did not stop there long. We found the fire, some footprints, the cold remains of a fire and a few bits of detritus like food cans and paper wrappers.

We pressed on.

I wasn't concerned about Omar's tracking skills. I had heard that native guides were no good in motor vehicles. They were used to reckoning distances by the speed of a camel, and could make nothing of a car's speedometer. But Omar had spent plenty of time on western ships and in motor-cars, and he was familiar with all modern forms of transport. His reckoning was always dead accurate.

Of slightly more concern was Digger's absolute contempt for compasses. Enough dirt and scratches had built up on the face of the compass in the lead vehicle that absolutely nothing could be made of it, and when we paused to eat at one point, I challenged him on the subject.

"Truth is," he replied, between mouthfuls of canned meat, "magnetic north is about as much use as an ashtray on a motorcycle. The steel in the lorry fair stonkers a compass—it'll be fifteen degrees off, sometimes twenty."

"So how do you get a bearing?" I asked.

Digger's face twisted into an expression of deep stress. "I don't rightly know, Mac," he admitted. "I think it's something to do with the height of the sun and the angle of the shadow cast by the radiator cap."

"You are as good as a Bedouin, effendim," commented Omar, a twinkle dancing in his eye.

Digger muttered something under his breath I couldn't catch, which seemed to be about the kind of people who would eat dingoes.

On the third day of our travels through the dead world, towards nightfall, we saw some dark blobs ahead of us. My heart soared at first, thinking they might be Assumpta and Br. Osvaldo; but then they began to elongate, until they became a cluster of tamarisk trees and date palms around a wide depression in which lay a small waterhole.

Parking the lorries at the top, we unloaded the cooking gear, unfurled our bedrolls, lit a fire and replenished our canteens. Taking several bags out of his own luggage, Omar lit a fire and began to mix a dough out of flour, water, and salt, and kneaded it on a flat rock. Soon, his arms were white to the elbows.

I took a dry branch and moved to throw it into the fire, but Omar stopped me. "No, effendim, please allow the fire to burn down."

I nodded, realizing that he wanted to use the fire for an oven. Sure enough, when it had burned to embers, he put the flat cakes he had made into them and covered the tops with more embers.

After this, Omar rose and examined the ground and concluded, "Excellent news, effendi: those we pursue were here less than twelve hours ago. We should catch up with them on the morrow."

"I think that calls for a celebration." Digger rose from where he had been heating some bacon and baked beans over a paraffin stove, and fetched a bottle from his own lorry. It was white wine.

"Sorry, Omar," said Digger, splashing wine into our tin cups, "I guess you don't touch plonk like this, do you?"

Omar inclined his head. "I should enjoy a glass of wine, I think, Dawkins-bey."

There was some eyebrow-raising at the campfire as Digger poured Omar a generous measure of wine. "Do not be offended, effendi," said Omar, "but I do enjoy wine, although I will not eat the flesh of a pig, and I do not enjoy food out of metal boxes." He made a slight grimace. "Metal boxes are for bullets, or for petrol, not for food."

Omar took out his knife and scraped the embers off his loaves, which he drew out of the fire and further scraped the blacked and charred crust away. He held out the loaves to us, and we all politely took a piece. It was unleavened, of course, but crisp, firm and delicious, especially with cheese.

A wind out of the north picked up. We shivered and huddled closer to the fire.

"Pardon me for saying so, Omar," I said with a quiet cough, "but isn't drinking the fermentation of the grape strictly against your religion?"

Smiling, Omar took an appreciative sip of the wine. "Inebriation is a bad thing," he explained, "for it prevents a man from fulfilling the will of Allah, the merciful, the just." His eyebrows furrowed slightly. "You are quite right, El Cracken. My religion forbids me from drinking of the fermentation of the grape or wheat, but I have fallen away from the religions of my fathers."

"In what way, if that's not too private a question?"

"It is not, effendim," answered Omar. "It is an honour that you ask." He thought for a long moment before beginning his story. "When I was but a small child," he said, "I accompanied my father on a visit to Barqua. During our trip, we visited a mosque, where the imam was revealing the truth to the faithful. He sat upon a little carpet, and they all listened to him, rapt. I listened too for a while, and realized that they spoke with great reverence about a woman.

"'O my father,' said I, 'of what woman do they speak?' I had never heard anyone in our tribe speak with such reverence of a woman.

"'Be quiet, small one,' answered my father, laying his finger upon his lips. 'It is Miriam, Mother of Isa, the Purified, of whom they speak.'

"This Isa is the prophet whom you all acknowledge."

"Jesus?" I said in surprise.

"The same, whom we call Isa, and his mother Miriam. To continue: 'O my father,' I said in what I took to be a quieter voice, 'forgive my question, but why do they speak of her with such reverence?'

"'O son of many questions,' replied my father, 'she is the worthiest of all women, the keeper of chastity, and her son Isa was the greatest of all prophets, only excepting Mohammed himself, the Prophet, the Chosen One of God.'

"'O my father,' I said again, 'forgive thy unworthy son if he troubles thee with yet another question, but was Miriam the Purified told, as my respected Mother is, that she might not join the menfolk at their meat, and that she must be veiled as my Mother is when she walks outside, and that she must walk ten paces behind her husband, as my Mother does?'

"At this, my father turned me around and held me quite firmly by the shoulders and I feared he would strike me, and turned my cheek away from him. But he dropped to one knee so that he could address me man to man. 'O beloved son,' he said, 'you have been listening to the gossip of women. Our wives must be veiled because we respect them more than our brothers or other men, not less. Their beauty is not for other men's enjoyment. A woman's beauty is for her husband, and for Allah the Just, who formed her in the beginning, as the Prophet tells, may he be praised for ever. Miriam the Chosen One of Allah is as if she were the mother of all men. She is above reproach. So is your Mother, O curious one.'

"He said no more, but a burning was in my heart at his words, and I longed for the answers to many questions. Another time, when I had grown to manhood, I went again to Barqua, and sought the same mosque, and found the same imam, now greying, sitting upon the same carpet, now a little worn. And I listened to his wisdom, and loved truth above all things. And as the day passed, and I stayed and listened to his words, the imam began to look at me until, late in the afternoon, he beckoned me and said, 'You seem to be one who seeks truth, O youth. What is it thou wouldst know?'

"And I told him what my father had said to me, many years before. At the end of my tale, the imam took a copy of the sacred book, opened it, and read from it, words I have laid in my heart and repeated to myself ever since: 'And Allah the merciful said to Mohammed the Prophet: "Tell in the Book of Miriam, how she withdrew from her family to a place in the east. Then We sent to her Our Angel, and he appeared himself to her as a well-proportioned man.

She said, 'Indeed, I seek refuge in the Most Merciful from you, so leave me if you should fear Allah.' He said, 'I am but the messenger of your Lord to tell you of a pure boy.' She said, 'How can I have a boy while no man has touched me and I have not been unchaste?' He said, 'It is thus: your Lord says, "It is easy for Me, and We will make him a sign to the people and a mercy from Us. And it is a matter decreed."' So Miriam conceived, and went with the boy into a remote place." Young Man of Questions, this is why we revere Mother Miriam: she is *Qanitah*, the most submissive one to the will of Almighty Allah. She teaches us the Way of Submission.'

"I thought much about the imam's words, but something did not sit well in my soul. If Mother Miriam were so great a person, why was her son only the *second* most important prophet? No such miracle attended the Prophet at his birth; why Isa, the second greatest prophet? I did not receive an answer for many more years, and when I did, as your honours have most likely guessed, the answer came from a Christian."

"So, you're a Christian, Omar?" I was full of wonder. "All this time, I had no idea."

Omar frowned. "Think no ill of your servant, effendim, but I have not yet accepted all Isa ibn Miriam says in your writings. Your Prophet Luke tells the same story as is told by the Prophet Mohammed. But there is this difference. In the story Mohammed tells, Allah commands Miriam to bear a child; it is a matter decreed. In your writings, it is Miriam who gives *permission for this to happen.* When I found this—that Miriam was not merely respected, but one to whom Allah Himself bowed in submission—I could not stay with my people. I knew I must reason the thing out in my own heart. So I did not return to my people, but made my way to Cairo, where I have lived ever since, helping, guiding, protecting people as they come to visit this land. I have spent much time in prayer, in mosques but also in Christian churches, and I have read much. Why did Allah, the great, the powerful, creator of the universe, submit Himself to the decision of a woman?"

"The answer's clear," I said. "Love."

"Love," repeated Omar. He sipped his wine. "I do not even know what is this thing, *love.* My father, I believe, loved my mother. I love this wine. And Allah loved Mother Miriam. There are many things to be said about *love,* and they do not go together in the usual way of words. I pray Allah will reveal it to me, but He has been most silent."

"Sometimes," I said, "you don't hear direct from God, but through men and women."

Omar gave an ironic smile. "Is there man born of woman who loves this way?" he asked. "If there is, I have not yet met him." He paused, staring into the fire. "Though sometimes, effendim, when I see you with Mrs. McCracken, or with the little ones,

Archimedes and Rosamund, perhaps I see there a glimmer."

Suddenly, Valparaiso raised his head and held up a hand. "Do you hear something?" he asked. "Something moving?"

We strained our ears. It seemed impossible—the whole world was dead. Bus as we listened, there did indeed seem to come a sound on the other side of the hollow, a rhythmic, scraping sound as if some rough beast were slouching through the desert sands.

And it was coming towards us.

Chapter 9
A Camel and a Truck

Valparaiso and I drew our revolvers. Digger picked up a shotgun. The satisfying click told us that he was ready for action. Throwing the end of the jerd over his shoulder, Omar led us away from the campfire and towards the noise.

It sounded as if it were about the size of a small dog, and it moved jerkily, pausing a moment and then shuffling on. Did it have rabies? I wondered. What on earth could it be? A cold, creeping feeling rose up my spine.

Digger switched on his electric torch; it lit up nothing other than the stony ground. But Omar, sheathing his curved dagger, stepped past us and through the yellow pool of electric light. We could just see his outline on the further side of the pool, bending.

Omar laughed. He put his hands on his hips, threw his head back, and guffawed to the icy stars.

"What is it?" Valparaiso asked.

"It is nothing, effendi," answered Omar, holding up something like a bulbous wig. "It is merely *a'kub.*"

"Tumbleweed?" said Digger, his voice sounding relieved.

Omar tossed it into the pool of light, where the wind caught it, and it began at once to roll away again. "It has come a very long way, sowing its seed where they will never grow."

Laughing, we returned to the campfire and began to settle down for the night.

I spent a long time before sleep, staring up at the sparkling sky above me. For some time, I reflected upon that lonely tumbleweed, earnestly fulfilling its mission to scatter it seeds far and wide.

Even in this lifeless place, I thought, there's life. And there's hope—as remote as it is, there's hope. It occurred to me that the tumbleweed had now passed through a small oasis. There was a chance some of its seeds might grow here.

I made the Sign of the Cross and, moments later, was asleep.

We rose before the sunrise, when it was still freezing cold, packed our belongings, extinguished the fire, and cranked up the lorries. We moved off through the grey and purple shadows cast by the mountainous dunes all around.

After about two hours of driving, I chanced to look over my shoulder. The dark dunes behind us were fringed with gold, which, as I watched, slid like a liquid down the near sides of the dunes until what had been dark was transformed, within seconds, to slopes of burning gold. I gave a gasp.

"Does the sunrise in the Sand Sea always happen so suddenly like that?" I asked.

"Pretty much," answered Digger. "You're wondering why? It's because the side of every sand-dune is always the same gradient, about thirty-five degrees."

"I see," I replied. "Sand begins to flow at thirty-five degrees, so dunes can't get any steeper than that."

"You got it, cobber. So when the sun reaches thirty-five degrees above the horizon, all the sand dunes light up at once, like Bourke Street on Christmas Eve. Strewth!"

Digger hunched forward, peering into the sands ahead of us. I couldn't see anything, but Digger slowed the lorry down so that, a few hundred yards later, we rolled to a stop beside the cold remains of a campfire. The other lorry, driven by Valparaiso, trundled up beside us, and Omar stepped down onto the sands.

"Easy to see what happened here," remarked Digger.

"Yes, effendim; they turned north."

"But why?" I wondered.

"We won't find out unless we follow them," Digger pointed out, and we got back into the trucks, turning their noses into the north.

We drove on for another few hours, until the sun began to descend on our left hands. Then, grinning, Digger pointed. Something dark was growing slowly in the sand ahead of us.

"Is that them?" I wondered.

"It's no group," Digger assured me. "It's one person, probably on a camel."

It didn't take long to catch up, because whoever rode ahead of us heard our approach and paused to allow us to catch up.

"Do they want to be caught?" I wondered aloud.

"I think that's *she*," answered Digger, his eyes narrowed. "What'd you say her name was?"

"Assumpta Bevan."

And indeed, as we drew near, it turned out to be Assumpta. She still wore the khaki skirt and blouse, with the pith helmet, but as she rode towards us on her camel, I could see that her face was back to its accustomed shape. When she spoke, I could see why.

"Good morning to you, Mac," she said, smiling; and I could see that those long teeth she had worn as Ramona Fortescue had been false. Her real teeth were a normal size, white and even. "So, you caught me at last!"

* * *

We were in the middle of the Great Sand Sea, a hundred miles from civilization. The international jewel thief had been caught at last. She eyed Chesterton Valparaiso with deep suspicion, but I could see in her eyes, she knew there was no escape—at least, for the present.

"So, we reckoned you weren't alone, Miss Bevan," said Valparaiso. "What happened to the monk you was with?"

"He took off in the night, with the guide. I woke up this morning, and the map was gone, the Staff was gone, the key was gone, the manuscript, and all the provisions. He even took the camels I rented in Aswan. You can't trust anyone nowadays."

"No," remarked Valparaiso, "you never know who might turn out to be a thief."

"I followed them at first. But that was a wan hope, without provisions. I was about to turn around and try to go back to Egypt. And then you turned up!"

"Well, Miss, this is not a rescue," Valparaiso assured her. "I'm here to put you in custody and take you back to the States for trial. Your days of crime are over, lady."

"You're so brave," rejoined Assumpta. There was something quietly defiant in her voice, and I was immediately suspicious.

"Effendi," said Omar, gazing up at the sky and sweeping his eyes along the western horizon, "we must make haste. A sandstorm is coming."

We hurriedly remounted the lorries. Omar took the camel, as he said it would be easier to track from the beast than from one of the motor-vehicles.

The northward track led to the ridge of a sand dune, so I drove with Assumpta in the passenger seat. Valparaiso rode with Digger.

I was used to climbing the sand dunes by now, and Assumpta showed no fear as we drove through the golden wall of sand and to the ridge, three hundred feet above.

Smiling, she turned to me and said, "It's been a long time, Mac. How have you been? I caught a glimpse of little Archie—my, how he's grown up!"

I grinned back. "Well, we went to Russia, and we spent the winter in Scotland. That was an exciting time." We rode in silence for a few moments. "I can't believe I didn't see through your disguise this time."

"Not like you did in West Africa!"

"Wait—I didn't get a chance to confront you back then. How did you know I knew you weren't who you said you were?"

Assumpta gave a lop-sided grin. "Your attitude changed very subtly after the night of the shipwreck. I guessed you must have seen me getting the golden idol statue back. After that, I was looking for the first opportunity to get away."

"There must have been plenty of those."

She nodded. "There were, but . . . well, I was enjoying myself." She sighed.

"So you're an international jewel thief!"

"I prefer the term *Lady Adventurer*, Mac. I'm not after money, just the excitement." Her face split in a wide grin. "When I saw you in Elephantine, I knew there was some adventure brewing. But I also thought you'd see through my disguise, so I had to get away—just not too far."

"How did you come up with the idea of Ramona Fortescue?"

Assumpta shrugged. "I ran into a young woman called Rosita Forbes in Asia last year, when I was after a pair of yellow diamonds called Oriental Sunrise. I tracked them all the way from Sotheby's in London to Hong Kong."

"Did you get them?"

"Of course, and substituted a pair of cheap imitations. I thought they'd do well enough to fool people until I'd made my getaway, but I missed the boat and had to book a trip a week later. There was plenty of suspense while I waited, but it did give me the chance of stealing a landscape by Dong Yuan."

"Do you still have them?"

"No, the diamonds and the picture were both too hot to keep. I left them in the houses of the curators of the museums I'd stolen them from."

I nodded. "And now it's over."

"Well, we'll see about that. Never say *Die*!"

Shortly afterwards, a hot wind began to pick up. I raised the windscreen, but it still blew in from the sides, bringing with it heaps of whirling sand so that our eyes stung and the coarse stuff filled our pockets and every nook and cranny of the vehicles. We were completely blind. Digger turned on his lorry's lights, so that I could see his red tail-lights, eclipsed from time to time by the twisting clouds. We didn't dare talk, because as soon as we opened our mouths, they would fill with sand.

Then, all at once, the lights of Digger's lorry vanished. I stopped our vehicle at once. I didn't have to brake—we were going slowly enough. I stood up, and found that in doing so I had lifted my head above the sandstorm, and could see quite clearly in all directions. I could see nothing of Digger's lorry.

"What's happened?" Ramona had to cup her hands about her mouth so it wouldn't fill with sand.

"I can't tell!" I replied. "Stay here—I'll go and look for them."

I jumped down to the ground, and waded through the storm a few yards, covering my mouth with a scarf, my arm held before my eyes. It was like getting a sand-shower, though I thought perhaps the wind was slackening a little.

Then a dark shape emerged from the brown maelstrom. It was Omar, leading the camel.

"It is the motor-lorry, effendim!" he yelled, as loud as he could, into my ear. I could barely hear him over the howling of the wind. "The honourable Mr. Dawkins drove it too close to the edge, and it rolled over."

"Is anyone hurt?"

"I have not looked yet."

But it was not hard to find. In tumbling down the side of the sand-dune, the lorry had shed petrol-cans, tins of food, bedrolls, and other supplies left and right. At the end of the trail, the vague shape of the lorry lay on its side like a beached whale. One human form stood off to one side, and the other arose from behind the stricken vehicle as we approached.

"Is it all right?" I asked.

Digger shook his head. "No-hoper," he said. "She broke the fore axle falling down the slope and ruptured the petrol tank. We've lost a whole tank of petrol, just soaking into the sand. The repairs would take a day in an equipped workshop, and we're over a hundred miles from the nearest one. Strewth, I could kick my own a . . . head, 'scuse my language, if only I could reach it! I'm as mad as a frog in a sock."

"Then . . . " I let my voice trail off. Only one vehicle and a camel. Five people. There couldn't possibly be enough room in one truck for four people and the supplies we would need. "You think we'll have to go back?"

"I don't think we have a choice." The four of us sheltered from the wind behind the lorry. "But this desert hasn't beaten me yet. When Australia and the world thought Digger Dawkins was dead, he managed to crawl out of this stinking armpit of a place. I say, we go back to Aswan, but leave most of our stuff here as a kind of supplies-dump. Omar, you can find your way back here, can't you?"

Omar had been looking around as if listening to something on the wind. But Digger recalled him to the present. "My apologies, effendi—I think the storm is calming. Yes, I can find this place again, and by the will of Allah can follow the trail again. These Romans drop their trash everywhere. It is—what would you say, effendim Digger?—no hard yakka."

"So, we leave, go back to Aswan, come back in two lorries, pick up our supplies here, then follow the trail to Zerzura!"

"That's a great plan, Mr. Dawkins," said Valparaiso, "don't get me wrong, a great plan. But do you think we ought to talk to *them* first?" He jabbed a thumb over his shoulder. We all looked up the slope.

"Holy dooley!" remarked Digger.

There, at the crest of the dune, were about a dozen men mounted on horses, wrapped in flowing robes and sporting old Martini rifles. Another four held Assumpta, in the good lorry, at gun-point.

"The Senussi," said Digger, raising his hands above his head. "Looks like we're well and truly stonkered."

The tribesmen eyed us maliciously. Their faces were dark, their teeth jagged, their skin seamed with age and weather. One of them shook his reins and his horse took a couple of paces forward, then stopped, tossing its mane. The man said something in harsh-sounding Arabic.

"What did he say?"

"I don't know," confessed Digger. "I don't talk Senussi—they killed too many of my mates in the war. Omar, d'you know the lingo?"

The corner of Omar's mouth gave an ironic twist and he bowed. "I shall endeavour, effendim." Turning towards the newcomers, he stepped forward. Instantly, a startled reaction shook the horsemen, and one of them cried out, "Omar al Mukhtar!"

"Do they know you, Omar?" I asked.

Omar nodded. He took a deep breath, as if he were about to reveal something important but embarrassing. "These are my people, the Senussi. I am one of them. This is Metwallah bu Jaghbub, a childhood friend of mine. Now, he serves Sa'ad bu Jibrin, Sheikh of the Wadi Buma." He paused. "That is where I was born, effendi."

"You're a Senussi?" Digger couldn't have looked more offended if he'd turned out to be a crocodile.

Omar fixed him with those dark, penetrating eyes. "Two tales are told of the war in the Great Sand Sea, effendim. Our losses also were great." He tuned back to Metwallah and spoke in Arabic. Metwallah replied, and the conversation went on for a while. In the end, he turned to me. "I have asked them if they have seen any Romans in these parts. I described Osvaldo-bey as near as I could, without having met him. Metwallah bu Jaghbub has seen no one, but he thinks our sheikh, Sa'ad bu Jibrin, may know something."

"Will he take us to him?" I asked.

Omar drew a deep breath. "I shall ask him, effendim. But do not hold out much hope. My leaving the Wadi Buma was not a parting in friendship. Metwallah is as likely to cut our throats as help us."

The conversation resumed. It involved much gesturing with the arms, shaking of the heads, and raised voices. But at last, Omar turned back to us. "Metwallah has agreed to take us to Sa'ad. This will be a journey of five days, for the Wadi Buma is in the Jebel Akhdar."

"The Jebel Akhdar?" I asked.

"The Green Mountains, where much rain falls. These are the fertile valleys the Romans have stolen from us. But there are places on the southern slopes that the Romans do not yet wish to turn into fields. It is good grazing land, and Sa'ad owns many cattle." Omar cast a glance up the dune at the horsemen. "I shall watch this Metwallah like a hawk. I do not trust him any longer. He has given his word, but that may not stop him cutting our throats anyway."

"Well, how do you like that?" Valparaiso said. "Seems there are more crooks in this desert than in Chicago."

And, under the watchful dull eyes of the Senussi's rifles, we re-packed the good lorry for our trip to Wadi Buma.

CHAPTER 10
THE SHEIKH OF WADI BUMA

And that's how our five-day detour into the north began. Assumpta and I rode a pair of horses vacated lately by Senussi who had been killed in a skirmish with the Italians. Omar rode the camel. Digger and Valparaiso drove the remaining lorry. The Senussi rode on all sides of us. There was no way to escape, even if there had been some place to which we could flee.

For the most part, we traveled at night, stopping in the late morning, when the heat became too oppressive. Then Metwallah would call for a halt, and we all built shelters, ate some bread like that Omar had made, and slunk inside our shelters to sleep. The best sleeping spots were under the lorry, which smelled, but shielded us well from the oppressive heat of the sun. When we rose, we packed our camp, and climbed back onto beasts or into the lorry. The back of the lorry began to be more spacious as we traveled further, ate the provisions, and used the petrol. In the end, a couple of Metwallah's men rode in the back, while a couple of the others led their horses.

We made our way through the dunes of the Great Sand Sea for another couple of days. Then the ground became harder, until we found ourselves faced by a stony, barren wilderness, where greyish tufts of grass clung tenuously to their waterless lives. Digger stopped our caravan and re-inflated the tyres of the lorry. After a couple more days, we began to see scanty trees among the bushes, and the ground began to rise. Before long, we moved among evergreen oaks and along the bottoms of wadis, up and ever upwards. The air cooled, and became in fact quite delightful. Metwallah changed our schedule so that we traveled in the daytime and rested after sunset.

Night had just fallen on the fifth day when Metwallah held up his hand and we all dismounted among dim trees and rocks. Overhead, the Milky Way sparkled and shimmered; the stars are brighter nowhere than in the desert. I could hear dogs barking in the distance, and the hoot of an owl. Omar's smile flashed in the darkness. "An owl—what we call *buma*. That is why this place is called Wadi Buma." He breathed in deeply. "Ah! The air of my childhood! It is very sweet!"

Chattering incessantly—he was now our firm friend—Metwallah led us to the entrance of a large tent. I had to duck to get through, and then found myself in a small hall, curtains rolled up to allow the night breeze to enter. Wooden sofas covered with carpets and pillows stood around the room, and we could hear the voices of women and children through a flimsy partition. Light came from a pair of oil lamps suspended from the roof-beam. They swayed gently in the breeze, so that the shadows swung back and forth.

The partition stirred, and a man in his late forties entered. Swathed in a white jerd, his wide girth was encircled by a belt into which was thrust a curved dagger in a jeweled scabbard. His curly beard was greying, and his eyelids were heavy, giving the impression that he was about to fall asleep. He leaned upon a tall and slender staff.

Omar bowed so low, his nose almost touched the carpet. He began to speak, but Sheikh Sa'ad bu Jibrin silenced him with a motion from one weary hand.

"Omar al Mukhtar," he said, "long has been your absence from Wadi Buma and you are welcome here. But I speak English, and need no interpreter." He made a wide gesture. "Sit and accept the hospitality of the desert."

As we took our places on the wooden sofas, a young boy about six years old, evidently one of Sa'ad's sons, brought around a large basin containing sour milk from goats and ewes mixed together.

"Ah, leban!" beamed Omar, smacking his lips and drinking deeply.

"May Allah refresh your soul, Omar al Mukhtar, have you then missed leban?" I could not see Sa'ad's eyes, for they were heavily lidded, but there was a faint smile upon his lips. “Perhaps you should have returned to us sooner—it would have been a comfort to your mother.”

Omar looked pained, and passed the leban to me. I was astonished at how refreshing it was, and began to feel a little stronger.

When we had all taken a draught from the leban, Sa’ad said, “Metwallah bu Jaghbub, may Allah preserve him from shame and harm, tells me you seek the oasis of Zerzura.”

On our journey, Omar had briefed me on how to address the sheikh. “Yes, Sa’ad pasha, may the blessings of God be upon you. Many miles have we traveled, over dune and through wadi . . . ”

The hand went up again, a little more energetically than last time. “Many are the white men who have come over dune and through wadi to seek the lost oasis. The desert has swallowed some, the jackals others. Why are you different?”

“Different?” I stammered. My mouth was dry, and I wished someone would pass the leban my way. “The desert will not swallow me up, Sa’ad pasha, nor the jackals . . . ”

“Because you have a truck and a Senussi for a guide? The desert is wide, Cracken-bey. Were one thing to go wrong, you would perish. And were it not that Metwallah pulled you out of your accident, I think you would have perished when something went wrong with your other truck. Or perhaps I am wrong?"

"You are not wrong, Sa'ad, but we have tokens that will guide us."

"Tokens? Is it not wise that all who travel through the Great Sand Sea bear tokens with them?" Sa'ad leaned forward on his sofa. "Cracken-bey, Zerzura is a myth, a story Senussi women tell their children before bed."

"We have a map," I told him.

"Have? Where is it?"

"It was stolen from us."

Sa'ad gave a hoarse laugh. "No doubt you tracked the thief through the sandstorm that destroyed your truck, yes?"

"Yes!" I answered with enthusiasm. Then, realizing how naive I sounded, I added, "Omar was tracking them."

"It is true, O light of the desert," Omar said, "that your unworthy servant had lost the trail in the sandstorm; but he would have picked it up again, by the grace of Allah, the compassionate, the merciful, when the storm subsided."

Sa'ad said nothing in response, but regarded us, pondering, for a long while. Then he gave a sigh. "Effendi, I cannot help you find Zerzura. But I can offer you hospitality while you are in my tents, and I can assist you in your return to Masr—what you call Egypt. But might I suggest . . . "

He was interrupted by a long, doleful wailing from behind the partition that sounded neither human nor animal, but something in between. It was most like a cat's night-time screech. Then a woman's voice cried out, "How dare you!" She followed this up with a stream of invective that I can't put into print. At almost every syllable, Sa'ad flinched, but Digger sat up straight on his sofa, his ear cocked.

"Barbs?" he said breathlessly; then, a little louder: "Barbs, that you?"

Whatever commotion had begun behind the partition was instantly stilled; Sa'ad's eyes, hitherto so droopy, were now intently fixed on Digger. Some inscrutable calculations were going on behind them.

The partition stirred, and a woman's face appeared. A veil covered the lower half of her face, but her eyes were blue and a wisp of blonde hair had escaped from the hem of the hijab. "Darling, is that you?" Her accent was thickest Australian. "I thought you was dead!"

"Well, I was—I mean, I got left for dead," answered Digger. "Strewth, I never expected to see you again, Barbs. I thought you was married to a sheikh!"

"I am, darling—I'm married to this *animal*!" She snarled the last word, jabbing a thumb at Sa'ad, who unloosed a torrent of furious Arabic. "See, he don't even speak Aussie half the time!"

"Well, he don't have the privilege of having been born Down Under, Barbs. You gotta give him a chance."

"If I'd known you was lying about being dead, I would never have married this bushranger."

"Fair dinkum?"

"Fair dinkum, darling."

"Well!" Digger shook his head, as if to dispel all misapprehensions from it. "You can't get a fairer dinkum than that."

"What are you saying?" demanded Sa'ad.

Digger turned his best Australian lawyer on the sheikh. "Well, it seems, Mr. Bu Jibrin, that the lady ain't entirely satisfied with the deal she got marrying you."

Sa'ad looked momentarily confused, then his face clouded and he roared, "Not entirely satisfied? She is wife of sheikh—sheikh who has many cattle, and house in Aswan. Many camels!"

Digger brushed a few specks of the desert from the lapel of his rather ragged jacket. "So, can I assume you're perfectly happy with the deal? 'Cause if you ask me, I'd say you ain't exactly grinning like a shot fox over it."

"Grinning like what?"

"Never mind. Are you happy being married to this lady?"

Sa'ad fumed. I could almost see smoke rising from his ears. "She talks too much, and she always argues."

"I do not!" yelled Barbs.

"In fairness, Barbs, you do," Digger corrected her.

"I don't think I do."

"Talk, talk, talk, all the time," sobbed Sa'ad. "I cannot stop her." In total defeat, he collapsed onto his sofa and put his head into his hands.

Digger knelt down beside the sheikh and said confidentially to him, "Would you care for an exit strategy?" Sa'ad nodded his head bleakly. Digger nodded his agreement. "I'll see what I can scrounge up, mate." Standing, he addressed Barbs: "It seems, Miss Barbs, that you have given your consent to this gentleman, which seems to me conclusive."

Barbs' hand flew to her chest in consternation. "I never gave him no such thing, Digory Dawkins, and how dare you suggest I would!" Her voice squeaked with indignation.

Angrily, Sa'ad too rounded on Digger. "I never touched her! Not once!"

Digger held up his hands defensively. "No, no, I mean, you gave permission. When you was married to this gentleman, you said, 'I do.'"

"Oh, I see," Slight pause. "Wait, I never did. I never said that. I just rode off with him into the night, like that Sherry Zady."

Digger whirled about to the sheikh. “Look, cobber,” he said, “I think I might be able to get you out of this, but I think there’s going to be a price.”

“Whatever the price, I will pay it!”

Digger winked at me. “Just you tell us everything you know about the lost oasis.”

Light went on behind Sa’ad’s eyes—the light of hope. “I tell you everything I know. And better—I take you there!”

When Digger turned around to face me and Valparaiso and Assumpta, his expression was not really like a shot fox, whatever that meant; but it was close to beatific.

Chapter 11
On to the Lost Oasis

Barbs and Digger sat on one of the sofas together, paying no heed to the rest of us, but giggling at a string of private jokes. Sa'ad looked at them in wonder.

"How is it that this Australian, who has no cattle, no camels, no house in Aswan, can make this woman happy, but I cannot?"

"It's love," Assumpta pointed out. Omar looked up, suddenly alert.

"What do they give?" Omar watched them, his brow furrowed.

"Give?" asked Assumpta.

"To love is to give," explained Omar. "What do they give?"

"I suppose they give themselves to each other," answered Assumpta, rather off-handedly.

Sa'ad gave a snort. "Love. I do not know what is that." His eyes narrowed. "But you have paid for something, Cracken-bey. Or your Australian friend has paid for it. Now I must tell you what I know about the lost oasis of Zerzura."

"What *do* you know?" I asked.

Sa'ad sat back on his sofa, and tore off a piece of bread, which he dipped into a mix of melted butter and ewe's milk. He said, "I regret I can tell you little, effendim. This Zerzura is a place Senussi women tell their children about at bedtime. There is in it—so the stories go—a weapon that I could use to drive these Romans, may they bear the curse of Allah, back across the sea to their homes. There was a story my father told me, and his father told him. Now I shall tell it to you."

Sheikh Sa'ad bu Jibrin chewed philosophically on his bread for a few moment, then began his story.

"O how the fortunes of good men have fallen since the days of my ancestors!" lamented Sa'ad. "I am but a poor man, with a tent in the Jebel and a house in Aswan, but the great-grandfather of my great-grandfather was the Emir of Barqua and, Allah praise him, a man of many cattle, many camels, and many palaces. When he was much the age that I am now, a traveler came to Barqua, spending much gold. My ancestor's slaves heard of this, because he spent not like a man accustomed to wealth, but like a peasant who by chance finds much buried gold. And so they apprehended him and brought him before my illustrious ancestor.

"'What is thy name, O thou vile and filthy thing, thou?' demanded my ancestor of the man. 'Tell me, by what chance camest thou to my emirate?'

"'O most worthy emir,' replied the wretched man, 'my name is Hamid Keila, and I am the owner of many cattle near Abw. But great hardship has

Allah, praised be He, visited upon me, no doubt for the schooling of my soul. Have mercy upon me, O great emir, and surely Allah the compassionate will have mercy on thee!'

"'Should Allah have mercy on me, or should he not, is no concern of thine. Say on. Why hast thou shown thy repellent face in my great and beautiful city? Thou art but dead unless thou answerest me, and answer true."

"'O truly wise and great emir, famed throughout the world for mercy, your servant is a trader, carrying ivory from Abw to Tarabolus. He started out from Abw with many companions and many camels, laden with the best ivory, taking the normal route.'

"'And what route would that be, vilest of worms?' demanded my ancestor.

"'The route that is customary among the family of this miserable slave, O most worthy emir,' answered Hamid, wringing his hands and trembling so that his teeth chattered, 'by way of the oases of Kargha and Dakhla. But as chance would have it, the third oasis to which we traveled, having been visited recently by another caravan, was dry.

"Then a great dispute fell out among us, for some of my men wished to return to Abw, others to go on, and that was what your servant wished. Some of them—though not this faithful but unfortunate one, Allah be praised—fell to blows, and some were slain. We went on, lamenting our fate to Allah the compassionate, the merciful. Some more of your servant's companions died. Then a great sandstorm arose, which your servant survived by sheltering under one of his camels. When the storm died down, the camel, alas, was dead.'

"'Many are the tales I have heard, for many are the years I have seen,' replied my ancestor, may his memory be honoured for ever. 'Thy tale is like many of them, and all are told by thieves. 'Master, I was lost in a sandstorm." There is no truth in them.' He signaled his executioner, who came forward, testing the edge of his scimitar on his thumb.

"Hamid cringed even more. 'If thy wisdom could see its way to sparing the life of this unworthy worm, O honoured one,' he cried, 'then thy servant would show thee what happened next—and what a wonder it was!'

"I will listen,' answered the emir, 'for the pleasant passing of the time. But if thou shouldst cease to delight me, thy death will be swift.'

"'Of course, of course!' whined Hamid. 'Behold now, O wise one, how your servant suffered. For did he not wander for days in the trackless desert, without food, without water, without his camels or his merchandise.'

"The emir yawned, and Hamid hastened on with his tale: 'He gave himself up as dead, believing that the desert birds would pick his bones clean. At last, he drifted off to sleep, but when he awoke, found himself in a tent, and being tended by men who were fair-skinned, with golden hair and blue eyes. They had found him and nursed him to life, and they took him to their home, which was a city in the midst of an oasis. At length, your servant escaped and came in a few days here, to this most hospitable and luxurious city.'

"The emir was long silent as he gave thought to what he had heard, and in the end he said, 'This city, did it have a name? I have never heard of a city where you describe it—there is nothing there but the empty desert.'

"'I cannot remember the name of the city, O honoured one!'

"'So you were not long there,' said the emir. 'They must have treated you abominably—show me thy scars, thy bruises."

"Hamid shook his head vigorously. 'No, O wise one, they treated me very well. I was a favoured son to them!'

"The emir's eyes narrowed. 'They treated you very well, yet you felt compelled to escape; and thou wert a favoured son, but thou didst stay for such a brief time thou rememberest not the name of the city.'

"Hamid was cunning enough to perceive his peril, and immediately said, 'I think the name of the city might have been something like perhaps . . . Zazzoo, or Zazuray, or . . . "

"'Zerzura!' cried the emir. At a snap of his fingers, one of his men stepped forward and searched Hamid until he found a ruby of magnificent size. The emir held it up, and saw that deep within it burned a fire, in its very heart. 'Thou hast not been honest with my, my friend,' he said. 'Thou must tell me where this city is, and lead me there. I hope, my friend, that if you choose to lie again, thou art not overfond of thy hands, for the scimitars are sharp in this palace.'

"When he heard this, Hamid's muscles quivered, his teeth chattered, and his throat grew too dry to swallow, so he led them into the desert, but there hid himself among the dunes, and was never seen again."

"Did he take the ruby with him?" I asked.

With a sigh, Sa'ad shook his head. "My ancestor, may Allah's mercy rest upon his soul, kept the ruby, but many years later, it disappeared, while another of my ancestors, Allah the merciful be just to him, was visiting Tarabolus."

"Tarabolus?"

"You would call it Tripoli."

I gasped. Tripoli! The pieces of the puzzle began to fit together. Reaching into my pocket, I held up my orichalcum stone. "Was the ruby like this?"

Sa'ad's eyes grew round and lit up as the oil lamps caught the facets of the Fire Stone and sent spears of golden light in all directions about the little room. “Where did you find this?” he asked, wondering.

“My father bought it in Tripoli, and it’s been in my family for many years,” I told him.

Sa’ad’s eyes narrowed. “Then you consider it to belong to you and your ancestors?”

I looked into the heart of the orichalcum, where flames seemed to burn. Omar watched me curiously. I leaned forward and placed the Fire Stone into the palm of Sa’ad’s hand. “It belongs to you, Sheikh Sa’ad bu Jibrin; my family was but for a few years its custodian. You have shown us great friendship in revealing these things to us, and I would not repay you by withholding what is yours.”

Sa’ad held the orichalcum up to the light. “El Cracken,” he said, “I have found honour in the heart of a Christian. For this, I shall do you a good act in return. There is one detail I have withheld from my tale, because my father, who passed the story on to me, told me, as his father had told him, to tell it to nobody except for a man of much honour, who would return what was lost to the Senussi.

“During the lifetime of the father of my grandfather, a traveler from the south reported seeing a city of white in the desert, far to the south. But he could not get in; the gate, on which was the image of a fabulous bird, was secured, and he could by no means open it. No one answered his call from within, but he found several pieces of gold in the sand outside the gates, which are now kept by my brother's family. When the father of my grandfather, guided by the traveler, led many camels south to the location of the city, he found it, but as the traveler said, he could by no means open the gate. If this is the city of Zerzura, which you seek, I can lead you there."

I inclined my head in respect and made the Salaam I had seen Omar make so often before. "Your generosity is as boundless as the desert, Sa'ad Pasha."

"But what good will this do you?" asked Sa'ad. "Or to me? Or to anyone? Can you open the gates which no man can open?"

"Well, we found a key," I said, "but I'm afraid it's one of the things that was stolen from us."

"Who has this key now?"

"His name is Osvaldo," I said. "He is an Italian—a Roman."

Sa'ad's eyes widened in alarm. "If he is Roman, then he must have taken the map and the key to the Romans, and they will certainly send many men, many soldiers, to find Zerzura. If they were to find the weapon that is hidden in the lost oasis, it would be terrible for my people! We would be driven out of the lands upon which our ancestors have lived for many generations."

"Oh, I wouldn't worry about that." We all turned in surprise, because Valparaiso had not spoken in a long while. "I don't think Brother Osvaldo has the key. What do you think, Miss Bevan?"

All eyes swiveled to her.

Assumpta looked at Valparaiso with a sour expression. "Well, I was going to volunteer it. But you have a keen eye, Mr. Valparaiso."

Reaching up, Valparaiso tapped his eye; it made a sound like tapping on glass. "Just one eye, but the good one can see a glint of gold in the shadow of a hat."

There was almost an expression of admiration in Assumpta's eye as she picked up her pith helmet, inverted it, and drew out the golden key we had taken from Bohemund's tomb. She dropped it into Valparaiso's outstretched hand.

"I see how it went," said Valparaiso. "You're in this caper for the fun—the harder the challenge, the better you like it. But this Osvaldo sap, he's in it for some political gain, right? For him, there's a higher purpose, one you don't trust."

Assumpta covered her surprise well. "You're very perceptive, Mr. Valparaiso."

"Well, it's how I make a living—two rooms overlooking an elevated railroad, gun hanging on the back of the door, dirty laundry hanging in the kitchen. It ain't much, but it's what I got. But you, Miss Bevan, we're talking about you, not me. When exactly did you switch those keys?"

"Br. Osvaldo never saw the real one."

Valparaiso nodded, grinning. He lifted his cigarette to his lips, then realized that he didn't have one and stubbed it out on the floor. "Yeah, that's about what I reckoned. So you took the fake key into the artifact room as part of your plan, concealed the real one, and gave the fake to the monk when you got out. Is that the way the fat lady sang, Miss Bevan?"

"I don't believe I'm a fat lady, Mr. Valparaiso."

"No, that you ain't, Miss Bevan. You ain't skinny neither. What you are is a pretty smart dame. You had this whole caper planned from the start, like a rabbit sizing up the lettuce patch."

"I don't know how you do it, Mr. Valparaiso," said Assumpta, "my congratulations."

"Well, one eye is good enough to see things—like the way you put your hat down, always brim-down, or the way you're always checking it to see if the merchandise is still there."

"So, are you going to arrest me?"

"Well, I sure have enough evidence to put you away in the Illinois State Penitentiary for a decade or two." He and Assumpta regarded each other for a long while in silence. Then Valparaiso handed the key over to me. "But I guess whether or not I turn you in depends, doesn't it, Miss Bevan?"

"On what, Mr. Valparaiso?"

"On your conduct over the next few days, Miss Bevan." He gestured to the Senussi in the tent. "It seems these people need your help."

Chapter 12
Shadows of War

It took a couple of days to organize our expedition south. Sa'ad would come with us, accompanied by his bodyguard of twenty Senussi. The five of us were to travel in the lorry and on horses; Barbs would stay in Wadi Buma until our return. The back of the lorry was piled high with supplies—somehow, Sa'ad managed to get many cans of petrol. When I asked where they came from, he made dark and incomprehensible noises; but I saw that they were all marked in Italian, and I guessed Sa'ad's men had raided an Italian supply depot.

Then, on the evening before we were due to leave for Zerzura, a man rode into Wadi Buma in great haste, leaping from his saddle before Sa'ad's tent-flap and throwing himself on the carpet before Sa'ad's feet. Sa'ad took the man away, beckoning Metwallah to accompany him, and we saw nothing of them for over half an hour.

We began to grow a little anxious, and wondered what could be the problem. Was there a situation that demanded Sa'ad's attention, and would take him away from our expedition south? We were discussing the possibilities when Sa'ad returned.

"Effendi," he said, "there has been a development that you should know. Many of my men hold positions of servitude among the Romans, and these men pass information on to me. Several of them confirm that the Romans have gathered a large army, about two thousand strong, with large cannon and cars with guns. Their intention is to march south and take Zerzura."

"So, Br. Osvaldo took what he'd stolen to the Italians, did he?" I gave a grim nod. "What do we do?"

Sa'ad took a seat upon his sofa. "I must gather an army. I cannot gather two thousand men in the time it would take these Romans to march here, but the Senussi can defeat an army larger than themselves, because they know the ways of the desert. But we must also secure what is in Zerzura. So, we will divide. Metwallah bu Jaghbub will remain here to gather the army. His task is to delay the Roman army in their march south, but *not to bring them to open battle.*" At this point, he glared at Metwallah, as if it were not the first time that evening he had made this point. "I and my bodyguard will ride south with you, to find this Staff of Zerzura." A mote of glee shone in his eye. "Then, I will use the Staff of Zerzura to destroy these Romans. The desert will be reddened with their blood, and the vultures will feast upon their bones!"

His sudden bloodthirstiness took me completely by surprise. But it was gone in an instant, and he was back to his usual jovial self.

The next morning, after a moving scene of parting between Digger and Barbs, who wailed that she hadn't ever been so upset since Digger hadn't died, the small column moved out along the bottoms of the winding wadis. The horsemen and the lorry were in the lead, the pack-animals behind. Sa'ad was resplendent in his dazzling white jerd, one of his older sons riding beside him with a parasol to keep him in the shade. Sa'ad's bodyguard marched on either side of the lorry, their ancient rifles shouldered, the bayonets none too sharp-looking. Omar, Assumpta and Valparaiso rode horses, the latter keeping his one good eye trained on the famous jewel thief. Digger kept his eyes fixed grimly on the path and spoke very little on that first day.

The sun passed overhead and then sank into the west, casting deep shadows across our path, and as we marched, it vanished behind the hills, leaving cool winds whistling through the valleys and the brilliant stars of ice over our heads.

As I was pouring petrol into the lorry's tank the following morning, Sa'ad and his son rode up to us in a cloud of dust.

"Effendi," he said, "the scouts have arrived. They say that the Roman army has moved out from Barqua."

"Will they catch up with us?"

Sa'ad shook his head. "An army cannot move as fast as a small group of men like us," he said. "Also, Metwallah bu Jaghbub will delay the advance of the army until we have the Staff of the Phoenix. That is what you call it, no?"

"Won't their scouts discover us?" asked Assumpta.

"Dead scouts report nothing," answered Sa'ad grimly.

After a short pause, I said, "Let's pray it won't come to fighting."

Sa'ad looked genuinely surprised. "Why, effendim? A man is made in battle!" His eyes narrowed and he leaned forward in his saddle. "You think because the Romans drive tanks and pull canon behind that they will not die? This is not France, effendim. These are Romans, and they do not know the desert as the Senussi do."

"So you have a strategy?"

Sa'ad nodded. "We will fight them as we fought the Frangi, in the time of my ancestors."

"The Frangi?"

"Those who came to take the holy city away from us—Al-Quds. What is it called in English?"

"Jerusalem," said Digger from underneath the bonnet of the lorry.

"Yes, *Jay-roo-salaam.* We will strike fast, then ride away into the desert, where their tanks cannot follow." He bellowed with laughter. "The sands will be dark with Roman blood!" Still chuckling to himself, he pulled on his reins and turned back towards his bodyguard.

Digger looked up from the lorry's engine. "I'll tell you flat, Mac, I don't care for all this talk of killing Europeans. Listen to all that yabber about men being made in battle and fighting over Jerusalem. I think our sheikh friend is stoked for a blue. He's as mean as cat's . . . er . . . teeth." Tipping his slouch hat, he added, "'Scuse my language, ma'am."

"You're excused, Mr. Dawkins," answered Assumpta.

I gave a sigh. "I think Sa'ad has a right to defend his homeland. The Italians shouldn't be here."

"I guess I'm just fed up with fighting." Digger closed the bonnet of the lorry with a clatter. "How about you, Mac? You served on the Western Front, didn't you?"

"I did, but only for a few days." Still, I thought, those days . . . my thoughts went back to the mud, the steel, the blood. I still couldn't hear a sharp noise, like a gunshot or a slammed door, without jumping a little.

We were underway a few minutes later. The fertile lands of the Jebel Akhdar gave way to stony desert, and then to sand, so Digger called a halt once more to deflate the tyres. Day after day unfolded, and we found ourselves traveling south along a valley between rocky heights on our right and tall dunes on our left.

News poured in about the Italian advance but, as Sa'ad had promised, their movement was slow, and Metwallah, with a mere three hundred Senussi, was able to harass them usefully, although they outnumbered him almost seven to one.

One evening, when it was still an hour until sunset, Sa'ad called for a halt. Beckoning me and Digger, he and a couple of his sons led us up a gulley and through a few twists and turns to the top of the rocky ridge on the western side of the valley. From the top, we could see the valley curving away southwestwards.

Sa'ad pointed. "Do you see those two peaks on the western side of the valley?" Lifting my binoculars, I could make out what he indicated. I handed the binoculars to Digger. "Between those peaks is a wadi that runs to the gates of the city that my ancestor, blessed be he in the sight of Allah, found. If that is Zerzura, we shall reach it early in the afternoon tomorrow."

"Starve the lizards!" said Digger. "So that's the place, is it?"

Sa'ad said something in Arabic to his sons, and this led to an extended discussion, culminating in a guffaw from Sa'ad. His eyes shining with good humour, he turned to us, and said, "You ask about strategy, effendim. We will draw the Romans down the wadi and trap them there, where we will kill them all from the cliffs. The desert will thirst no longer!" And laughing again, he led us back down the track to where the camp had already been built.

"What's going on?" asked Assumpta.

"We're a day away from the wadi that leads maybe to Zerzura," I explained.

Digger jabbed a thumb over his shoulder. "That digjam of a sheikh wants to set up an ambush for the Italians, if you'll pardon the expression, ma'am." Digger pulled off his slouch hat and wiped his brow. "It ain't like I didn't see enough of my mates die out here. I'm through with this kind of . . . rubbish."

"None of us wants to see the war continued here, Digger," I answered.

"I guess that's right," said Valparaiso. "Seems to me, though, this is the sheikh's business. It's his home that's been invaded. I don't reckon I'd like to see foreign soldiers marching through Chicago." After a pause, he added, "I guess there are some parts of Chicago I wouldn't recommend they invade."

It took me a long while to go to sleep that night, but I woke with a start at what must have been about three o'clock in the morning. I was surrounded by total darkness, and I could hear Digger's breathing beside me. I cast off my sleeping bag and crawled to the tent flap. Poking my head through it, I saw that I was in the last place I would have imagined in the whole world: I was on the Western Front.

It was a dream, of course, but I didn't know that at the time. I just crawled out of the tent and onto the wind-swept plain of mud. It was eerie, how there was nothing around, no people, no planes overhead. The blasted trees and the mud, they were there. I walked on, my bare feet making sucking sounds as I pulled them out of the mud.

I saw a dark scar in the earth ahead of me, lined with sand-bags and barbed wire. I vaulted down and found myself in a trench.

Two men sat on the firestep. One wore a British tanker's uniform, the other the field grey of the Imperial German Army. They both looked at me with recognition.

"Hamilton?" I said. "Willie Hamilton?"

Hamilton gave a nod. "Who'd have thought we'd meet again here, eh, McCracken?" He gestured to his German companion. "This is Armin Schultz, a friend of mine."

"*Guten tag, Herr McCracken,*" said Armin.

"Do you remember Armin, Mac?" asked Hamilton. At my obvious incomprehension, he said, "When we found our way into that trench, it was Armin here who attacked you."

I gasped. "You died!"

Hamilton and Schultz nodded. "Aye," said Hamilton, "I killed him."

Schultz clapped him on the back. "But that to me is no offence now, eh, *meine Freunde*?"

"I lasted a month after our adventure together, Mac," said Hamilton. "Then shrapnel got me in another tank. That Mark V-Star was never any good, was it?"

"Do you have something to tell me?" I asked.

"Aye, I do. You'll recall, McCracken, I canna give you too many details or any specific advice."

"Why not?" I asked. "Please, be specific."

But Hamilton shook his head. "It's all about free will," he said. "All I can say is, What did Our Mother tell the children?"

A wind began to blow off No Man's Land, and smoke funneled along the trench.

"Children? What children?" I coughed; the smoke cloyed my lungs.

"War's a damnable thing, Mac," said Hamilton. I could barely see him for the swirling grey clouds. "It saw to me and to my pal here. Think on Mary and the wee sproggins." He smiled. "Och, but will ye no ken that?" he said, pointing.

I followed where he pointed. In the midst of all the smoke, sunlight had touched some distant, bare hills.

"The sun danced in the sky at Fatima and in Siberia," said Hamilton, "and now sunlight lies on the dunes." But the smoke had almost totally concealed him. I fell to my knees, choking and covering my face with my hands.

"You all right, Mac?" The voice had an Australian accent. "You bloody well woke me up, you daft old pommie."

"Sorry, Digger," I said. "I was dreaming."

"Well," said Digger, turning over in his sleeping bag, "see if you can't dream a little quieter, eh?"

We set out again the following morning, still following the path southwards between the dunes and the mountains, until we came to the peaks Sa'ad had indicated. I had imagined them to be spaced pretty far apart, but that had been a trick of perspective. In fact, the gap between the peaks varied from about a ten-foot-wide tunnel at the foot to almost nothing at the top. It was almost as if the peaks leaned on each other, ne'er-do-wells in mutual need of support.

"No wonder no one could find this place," Digger commented. "All that desert, and look at that gap—narrower than an Englishman's mind. No offence, mate."

"None taken—I'm a Scot."

Sa'ad insisted on being the first to enter the wadi, and we had to wait, the lorry's engine idling, for him and his two sons. I looked at the dunes opposite. The sun was behind the peaks, which cast shadows across their near slopes. What would we see, I wondered, if we drove, using Digger's technique, to the top of that dune? Would we see anything of the lost oasis from there?

Sa'ad trotted—the hoofs of his horse almost pranced—towards the gap, flanked by his sons, one of whom carried the parasol. They entered, and the deeper darkness of the wadi swallowed them up.

"Right. Our turn." Digger threw the lorry into gear, the tyres spun, and we rolled towards the gap. Behind us, the horses, camels and men of Sa'ad's bodyguard moved after us.

We entered the tunnel, and were at once immersed in a delightful cool and an almost complete dark. Digger thumbed on the headlights, revealing level sand ahead of us, and dimly illuminating stone walls. The roar of Ford engine's four cylinders filled our ears. Looking up, I could see a strand of light, threaded with occasional beads—the irregular and extremely narrow gap between the two peaks.

Assumpta was riding beside us now. "Just a touch of sunlight!" she yelled, above the noise of the engine. "I feel quite giddy—as if just a drop of sunlight were enough to bring the whole mountain down on top of us!"

I nodded, but could say nothing in reply. The engine was too loud.

But one turn and then another brought us out of the tunnel and into a steep-sided valley, the sky a sleeve of brilliant blue above us. The walls were layered in reds, oranges, and pale yellows, and centuries of winds had scooped them out in wild patterns. If the winds could become visible, I thought, that's what they would look like, whirling and bowing and soaring by turns, pirouetting suddenly one way, gliding unexpectedly the other. And now, on either side, I could see tufts of grass, at first greyish, but soon plush little spears of pure emerald, and trees, sometimes leaning out over our passage at crazy angles, sometimes standing serenely against the walls of the wadi.

The wadi twisted and turned, and we drove along it, Sa'ad and his sons twenty yards ahead of us all the time, their steeds high-stepping, their bridles jingling. Behind us, the sunlight touched the ends of the bodyguard's old-fashioned bayonets.

Just a touch of sunlight. I frowned. There was something in that.

"Look!" Assumpta pointed. Ahead, through a narrow crack in the rock, we caught a glimpse of bronze geometric patterns—manmade and no mistake.

"It looks like we've found the bloody thing," I said, "excuse the language, Digger."

With a wink, Digger threw the wheel right then left, and we found that the wadi opened up into a wide valley with sheer sides, about seven or eight hundred feet high, red and gold cliffs festooned with thick tufts of grass and knots of tamarisk trees. Dead ahead of us rose a manmade wall, made smooth and even centuries ago, to which patches of whitewash still clung. In the midst of it stood a pair of brazen doors, into which was etched the image of a bird rising from tongues of fire. Its beak was curved like that of an ibis, on its head was a disk, and in each talon an ankh, that typically Egyptian symbol that looked like a cross with a loop at the top.

Drawing up alongside of Sa'ad, Digger killed the engine.

Assumpta pointed. "The ankh symbolizes life," she explained. "The disc on its head represents the sun—it's sacred to Ra, the sun-god. And the phoenix, according to legend, was always sacred to the sun-god."

"You know, Miss Bevan," commented Valparaiso, "you don't need to keep up your cover."

"I chose a cover that I'd enjoy," replied Assumpta. "I always wanted to be an archaeologist when I was a child."

"Beats being a jewel thief, I guess."

"Not very different at all," rejoined Assumpta. "How many of the treasures uncovered by archaeologists in Egypt have ended up in Egyptian museums? Not many."

Valparaiso gave a shrug. "Fair point."

"A bird that flies up from long grass," commented Sa'ad.

"I think what you imagine to be grass, Sa'ad, is in truth flames. The bird if a phoenix."

"Flames? Is it so, El Cracken?" I nodded, and Sa'ad let that sink in a few moments. "This bird is not wise, I think. But as you will." His lips expanded into a smile that looked cunning. "Behold, Cracken-bey—we have reached the lost oasis!"

Chapter 13
The Throne Room

We had found the city of Zerzura, or so we thought, but nobody moved for the moment. I waved my hat in front of my face, partly to cool me down, but partly to discourage the flies from buzzing about my face. Sa'ad crooked a finger to his sons, and the two of them trotted forward. A deep conversation in Arabic began between the three of them. It involved much pointing and other kinds of gesticulation.

Behind us, Sa'ad's bodyguard fell out. They dropped their rifles onto the sandy floor, folded their legs underneath them or just flopped down to sleep instantly. Some of them pulled rations out of their pouches and began to chew. Others talked. One pair opened a backgammon game. The soft rattle of the dice, multiplied by the near cliffs, seemed to echo from all directions. It sounded like dry bones rattling.

Sa'ad's conversation dragged on.

"We going in or not?" wondered Digger. "This yabbering could go on for ever."

"Omar!" I beckoned him over. He pulled on his reins and steered that beautiful white stallion over to us. "What are they talking about?" I asked.

Omar glanced at Sa'ad and his sons. "They talk of how they will defend this place against the Romans, effendi. They will block off their retreat, so that none of them may escape. With the Senussi hiding among the rocks all around, it will be easy to slaughter them all without taking any casualties ourselves."

I looked up at the cliffs around us. Was this place always in the shade? I wondered. The sun touched the rim of the cliffs, but none of it reached the floor—the killing-ground.

"Are you comfortable with this, my friend?" I asked Omar.

Omar took a deep breath. "It is the way of my people, Cracken-bey. You have told me that love always finds a way, but these men have not read the same books that you have read." At a sudden commotion behind us, we all turned around. One of the bodyguard was attempting to sit on another's head. "Indeed," remarked Omar, "few of them have read any books at all. Perhaps love will not find a way here."

"He will," I asserted. But how? I wondered. And when?

Sa'ad half-turned in his saddle and motioned for us to join him.

"Cracken-bey," he said, "we have been discussing how we may destroy all of the Romans who come here seeking the Staff of the Zerzurans. We have a fine plan!"

"This is a small place to fit two thousand men," I pointed out, motioning to the open space before the gates.

Sa'ad shrugged. "If Metwallah bu Jaghbub does what he is supposed to," he explained, "there will not be two thousand Romans left when they get here. It is the price they pay for taking lands that do not belong to them. But have you the key, effendim?"

I drew the three-lobed key out of the breast pocket of my shirt and held it out to him. It seemed bright in the shadows, as if it lit itself up. I turned my face upwards. There, on the gates, was the image of the phoenix.

"'Insert the Key of Zerzura into the beak of the Phoenix,'" I said slowly.

"Crikey!" imprecated Digger. "That must be twenty feet up, if it's an inch!"

"Do we have a ladder on the lorry?" I asked.

"Sure," answered Digger, "it's slung underneath, but it's only a twelve-footer."

There was indeed a ladder slung under the chassis of the lorry, suspended by an elaborate system of hooks and ropes that only Digger understood. In a few minutes, we had driven the lorry right up to the gates and rested the foot of the ladder on its bed.

The top rung was still a few feet from the beak, but I reckoned I could reach it.

Digger and Omar held the ladder fast and I snaked up it.

I was still a foot short, reaching as high as I could with the key. Gripping the raised image of the bird, I climbed up by another rung, and then another.

I've never really been afraid of heights, but the ground seemed to sway like the ocean below me.

But my eye was on a level with the beak of the phoenix, which formed an almost complete circle. In the middle of it was a keyhole.

My fingers sweating, I slipped the key out of my pocket again. Something was blocking the keyhole, and the key would not fit. I blew into the keyhole, and got a face-full of sand and dirt that made me cough and blink for a few moments. I reeled backwards a bit, and felt the ladder shift below me. Digger's voice came up to me: "Whoa there, boy!" And Omar: "Effendim! Have a care!"

I grabbed the raised edge of the phoenix image, my heart pounding. I waited, until I was sure the ladder wasn't moving under me any more. Then, rubbing the dust out of my eyes, I said a brief prayer of thanksgiving.

I tried the key again, and this time it fit perfectly. With a low click the wards turned and lined up. The gate shifted, the ladder moved, and my fingers curled about the edges of the bronze wings. My face was pressed against the gate.

"You okay up there?" yelled Digger.

"Mmm-mff," I answered.

Gingerly, I pocketed the key, then lowered myself down the ladder. My foot felt one rung then the next, and finally I felt confident and slid down the rest.

While Digger and Omar folded up and stowed the ladder, I sat in the back of the lorry, my hands shaking slightly. I had flown in aeroplanes in combat and in airships, I had climbed mountains. And this was the only time I had been afraid of heights—at a meagre twenty feet!

Digger moved the lorry, and Sa'ad marched up to the gate, giving his reins to a servant. He pushed one of the gates. It did not move. Several of his men hurried up and put their shoulders to it until, slowly, creaking like an old man, it opened inwards upon a darkened interior.

Snapping out something in Arabic, Sa'ad held out a hand. A soldier hurried up, lighting a torch and handing it to him. I took out my electric torch, and glancing at one another, we edged in through the doorway.

We were confronted by a huge pile of rubble, stretching all the way up to the broken ceiling above us. It was as if the whole mountainside had collapsed upon this point.

The next thing we noticed was the bodies: two dozen or so skeletons, most of them clad in medieval armour, lay stretched in various poses among the dust. One of them had been half-buried by the rock-fall. Some of them wore purple rags about them, others red and yellow.

Valparaiso strode forward and bent over the half-buried body. Then he stood and scanned the scene of carnage.

"I see everything that happened. These boys, the ones in purple, they was running away. Probably had the bejeebers scared out of them by something. And the guys in red and gold were after them, hot on their heels." He gestured with his unlit cigarette. "My guess is the red-and-gold boys were Zerzurans, and the guys in purple . . . "

"Saracens?" suggested Assumpta.

"I was going to say that. Saracens. So the jig was up for the Saracens, and they knew it. Then this Bohemund guy, he takes out the Staff of the Phoenix, and he uses it on them, and blows the whole side of the mountain to kingdom come. Right in the middle of the battle."

"But that doesn't agree with Bohemund's account in the manuscript," I pointed out. "He said he used the Staff of the Phoenix when the battle seemed hopeless to the Zerzurans."

"Sure, you can believe him if you want," replied Valparaiso. "You can believe the earth is flat if you want, or that the L train will run on time one day. It don't make a refried bean's difference. The evidence is clear. Looks to me like he stands to gain a lot if folks think he only used the crazy weapon in self defence. But this wasn't self defence. It was cold-blooded murder. Murder most foul."

"Or murder most fowl," I added, "if the phoenix was involved."

Nobody laughed at my joke, but there was a short pause.

"This was certainly the scene of a battle," Assumpta remarked, regarding the skeletons with a mixture of distaste and professional curiosity. "You don't see remains like this very often—usually, someone cleans up after the battle."

She made the Sign of the Cross and we followed suit, even Valparaiso. Sa'ad watched us with curiosity, a crease appearing between his eyebrows. But he said nothing.

I looked up towards the ceiling. About twenty feet from the ground, on each side, stretched a terrace, largely consumed by the rockfall.

"How do you suppose the Zerzurans got up there?" asked Digger.

"I'd bet the staircases have been covered up by the rockfall," I answered. "'And fire flashed forth, and the walls shook, and rocks from the mountaintops fell upon the city, and many fell dead in the streets.' This is part of the damage done by Bohemund with the Staff of the Phoenix."

"That's quite a popgun he had," commented Valparaiso.

At Sa'ad's bidding, one of his bodyguard advanced towards the pile of rubble. He began to pick his way up it, clambering from rock to rock, pausing as one shifted under his foot. Once, he slid back a foot, and a minor rockfall went rumbling down towards the floor. In the end, though, he reached the terrace above and grinned down at us.

Now that he saw it was safe, Sa'ad and his sons began the climb, and we all followed after them. I, for one, was a little frustrated by his lack of speed. He had to test every step with almost paranoid care, and his sons were ready to catch him if he stumbled a sixteenth of an inch.

In the end, Sa'ad reached the terrace, and raised his hands as if he had accomplished an athletic feat. We joined him moments later.

The terrace was twenty feet wide, littered with fragments of rock and masonry and a couple of skeletons. A pair of doorways led off it; there may have been others, but the rockfall had concealed them.

"We will go this way," declared Sa'ad, holding up his torch towards one of the doors.

We entered what appeared to be some sort of guardroom, scattered with bits of ancient furniture. On one wall was a rack on which a variety of spears and swords were arrayed. Shields hung on the walls. A mail shirt was draped on a frame in the corner. There was no exit.

The other door led through a series of rooms, some of which were filled or almost filled with fallen debris, like the entrance hall. In some of them lay more skeletons, sometimes dressed in armour, sometimes in fabric. Some wore turbans and were armed with scimitars; others wore robes of red and yellow, bearing straight swords. The dry climate had preserved them remarkably.

In one of the rooms, we found some stairs, down which filtered the blue light of outside. Climbing them one by one, we emerged into what had been another room, but was now open to the skies, the walls having collapsed and rolled away down the mountainside.

For the first time, we got a look at the whole city of Zerzura.

It was located in a roughly circular hollow between mountains that totally surrounded it. In the centre of the hollow was a lake, so impossibly blue you thought it could not be natural. Around the lake were a host of trees—not the grey things, clinging desperately to life that we had seen in the wadi, but rich, fertile, emerald-green trees dripping with life.

In the middle of the lake was an island, where more trees climbed up the sides of a building, whose cupola peeked out from among the leaves. Nothing else could be seen of it.

The city itself rose in concentric terraces from the lake, and houses had been carved out of the mountainsides along them. Many of them were now reduced to rubble. Most of them were missing the roofs. The ones that remained were flat, sometimes shaded by trees.

"This is Eden, without the Fall," said Assumpta.

"Oh, they fell all right," replied Digger. "Remember those skeletons back there?"

Assumpta made a wide gesture that took in the city, the trees, and the lake. "It's a paradise," she said, "but augmented by human accomplishment."

Valparaiso pointed. A bird, grey but with red flashes on its wings, swung from one tree to another—a parrot. Through the trees near the lake, we caught glimpses of the soft hides of gazelles. The sound of trumpeting came to us, and from behind one of the buildings emerged what looked like an elephant, but which was only a little larger than a large dog.

Assumpta nodded slowly. "So," she said, "a whole system of plant and animal life survived here." She pointed towards the trees and water. "There's everything they need here."

"But no people—they've all gone," I pointed out.

Sa'ad clapped his hands, and we all turned to him. "Effendi," he declared, "we must find the Staff of Zerzura. The Romans will be here soon—three days, perhaps only two!" And he clattered down the stairway, drawing with him his sons. Below, in the lost oasis, a herd of aurochs reached the side of the lake and lowered their heads to drink.

We went on through more passageways and rooms, finding more bodies, more broken or burned furniture, more collapsed debris from the mountain.

"The Fire Stone couldn't have done this much damage," I whispered to Digger and Assumpta. "I've used it—the one my Dad gave me."

"Perhaps there's something in the Staff itself," suggested Assumpta, "like a magnifying glass."

"Something that would increase the power of the orichalcum?" I said. I thought about it for a moment. "I don't know whether to be impressed or afraid."

We had walked a long way by this time, and on the next occasion that we found a window looking out over Zerzura, we stopped and drank in the fresh air.

From here, we could see the full extent of the rockfall. Rubble was heaped at the foot of the mountain, and for about a hundred yards on either side, rooms formerly carved out of the rock of the mountain had been blown open, their interiors exposed to sunlight.

"I've never seen anything do this kind of damage," I said to Assumpta. "It would take multiple direct hits from the largest artillery we have today, or a direct hit on an ammunition dump."

Sa'ad was looking at the damage from another window, and had clearly made the connections we had made. He caught my eye and rubbed his hands together, grinning like a child in a sweet shop.

Moving on, we soon found ourselves climbing a gentle incline towards double doors, once more decorated with the phoenix motif. This time, however, the keyhole was well within reach. And the key fitted. I turned it and pushed the doors open.

The inside was dark, but not without light. It entered through a circular vent in the roof. The whole room, in fact, was circular, with ranks of seats around the walls and a raised platform in the middle of it. The light from above lit up the platform, and the throne that stood upon it.

Upon the throne, a figure was seated. The figure wore a crown. A red and gold robe was draped about his shoulders. In one hand was a flail like the ones held by pharaohs.

In the other was the Staff of the Phoenix.

Chapter 14
Fire Bird and Fire Stone

Sa'ad's eyes shone in the flickering light from his torch. In an excited whisper that seemed very loud, he said, "This must be the throne room of which you spoke, effendim—and there is the Staff of Zerzura."

He took a step forward, but I put a hand on his arm. "Be careful," I said, "the place may be trapped."

"I see nothing!" He ran his eyes over the domed roof, the ranks of seats like a parliament, the glossy marble floor, and the platform. Turning to his bodyguard, Sa'ad announced: "A bag of gold to the man who will walk to the throne and back!"

One of Sa'ad's men stepped forward and rattled off some Arabic.

"Ahmed," said the sheikh, "has volunteered to fetch the Staff of Zerzura!"

Ahmed readied his rifle, his eyes peering left and right, glinting with the anticipation of much treasure. He stepped out into the throne room. The bayonet quivered. The figure on the throne glared with empty eyes at us. Ahmed walked cautiously on, his head turning left and right as he went.

All at once, an unearthly scream tore at our ears. A streak of yellow and red flashed through the air.

Ahmed screamed, casting aside his rifle and raising his hands to his face.

A huge bird, bigger than an eagle, had sunk its talons in him. Its plumage was russet and gold, and its beak was curved. It tightened its grip.

Suddenly, Ahmed's clothing darkened to black. His screams ceased as flames sprang out from his body. In moments, he dropped to the marble floor, dead, and the bird swooped away, up near the vent in the ceiling.

"I guess the room was trapped after all," observed Valparaiso. "Might have known in Zerzura they'd have a guard phoenix."

Sa'ad stamped his foot petulantly. "Shoot it! Shoot it!" he screamed.

Several of his soldiers rushed forward, knelt, and thrust the stocks of their ancient rifles into their shoulders. Shots boomed out, echoing in the cavernous throne room.

The bird swooped down once more, and fixed itself onto the chest of one of Sa'ad's men. The others hastily dropped bullets down the muzzles of their guns; one of them fumbled his ramrod and scrambled to pick it up.

The man seized by the phoenix reached for his dagger, but he could not loosen it from the sheath. Flames erupted from his chest, where the bird clung to him. He fell backwards onto the marble floor as the bird went winging off again.

The remaining men fired scattered shots after the bird.

A tapping sound came from beside me. One of Sa'ad's sons had loaded his rifle and tapped the stock against the stone floor to drop the bullet just a little lower. Calmly he raised the muzzle, fitting the stock into his shoulder.

The phoenix swooped down again, plunging its claws into a new victim.

Sa'ad's son took careful aim. He squeezed the trigger.

I had moved a little away from him, so when the shot crashed out, it did not make my ears ring.

With a scream, the phoenix threw back its head and released the man. It flapped its wings, but could gain no altitude.

The moment it hit the floor, a ball of flame exploded from it. The fire blossomed outwards, engulfing the survivors out in the throne room.

We ran. Flames gushed along the passageway, licking at the walls, curling about our heels. I pitched forwards, feeling a scorching heat on my back.

The fire died away, leaving the smell of petroleum behind. I got to my feet, my knees shaking. The walls, I saw, were blackened. Sa'ad still held his torch aloft. My shirt fell from my back in two singed pieces. We ran down the passageway to the entrance to the throne room.

I won't tell you of the sight that met our eyes there, except that, where the phoenix had been lay a heap of grey ashes.

"Well," said Assumpta, "I never thought I'd see that!" She made the Sign of the Cross.

"What's this," asked Valparaiso, "a thief with a faith?"

"A guardian of the law without one?" returned Assumpta.

Valparaiso opened his mouth to reply but changed his mind. "I never said I didn't have a faith," he answered quietly.

"What is this?" wondered Omar. Stooping, he brushed away some of the ashes to reveal an egg, about three inches long, and a pale gold in colour. A smile spread along half of Omar's mouth. "A phoenix egg!" he declared. With a quick glance at Sa'ad, whose attention was fixed elsewhere, he stowed the egg away in the folds of his jerd.

Sa'ad walked slowly towards the throne and, climbing it in a couple of steps, took from the hands of the long-dead King of Zerzura the Staff of the Phoenix.

* * *

Not long after this, we found a doorway that led out onto the mountainside. Sa'ad, the Staff in one hand, the Fire Stone in the other, led us up towards the mountain-peaks. After picking our way among rocky hills for a while, he paused. With a grin, he fitted the Fire Stone into a hollow at the top of the Staff of the Phoenix.

"Sa'ad, wait!" I yelled out. "Let me see if I can figure out how it works first."

Sa'ad handed me the Staff. "But I must be the first to fire it!"

"Of course, Sa'ad, of course." Popping the Fire Stone out for a moment, I examined the head of the Staff. The top was a large diamond, or more properly, a prism. Underneath it, the chamber into which the Fire Stone fitted was made of a silvery-white metal. From a hatch in the front a small handle projected. Pushing and pulling on this handle, I observed that an aperture on the front narrowed or widened.

I smiled. That was how the beam was controlled.

So what was the metal on the inside? Surely not silver. I tried scratching it, then held it close to my nose and sniffed.

At once, I held it out at arm's length. Sniffing the inside, I had tasted garlic at the back of my throat.

Tellurium! I thought. The garlic flavour was what was called "tellurium breath." Even in relatively small quantities, inhaling tellurium was toxic. Discovered about a hundred and fifty years earlier, it had been used to collect and concentrate the sun's radiation. So that was the Zerzurans' secret.

"What have you discovered?" asked Assumpta, closing in curiously. Everyone else gathered around too.

"Well, the prism on top refracts sunlight from any direction into this tellurium-lined chamber. There's probably some sort of power cell in the shaft here. It would make for a very powerful charge, which is directed out through this aperture on the front. You control the strength of the beam with this handle." I looked more closely at the shaft just under the head, and found, as I had expected, a trigger. "This trigger makes a connection with the Fire Stone. Even without the orichalcum, it would probably produce some kind of beam; with it, it would be extremely dangerous. Put it on the lowest setting possible. Be careful."

Sa'ad reached out. "I will try, El Cracken," he said. He placed the Fire Stone into the chamber and shut the hatch. Eyeing me briefly, he adjusted the aperture to the narrowest beam, held the Staff of the Phoenix out at arm's length and squeezed the trigger.

The familiar beam of light leaped from the Staff of the Phoenix with its loud crash and the smell of ozone. The beam hit the top of a rocky outcrop twenty yards away. The outcrop exploded, showering rock fragments all around. We all ducked.

When the debris had finished clattering all around us, we stood. Sa'ad beamed in delight.

"Many infidels will die!" he announced. He did a little dance.

"Sa'ad," I said, "don't use this weapon right now. It's very dangerous. Let us discuss how we will use it responsibly."

"Of course, Cracken-bey," he replied sheepishly. "You can trust me." He took the Fire Stone out of the chamber and pocketed it.

As we turned away from him, I saw Metwallah climbing up the rocky slope towards us. He gave us the Salaam as he passed us, grinning so we could see almost all of his teeth. At once, an intense conference began between Sa'ad, his sons, and Metwallah.

Digger gave a sigh. "This could go on for a while," he remarked.

Assumpta snatched a glance over her shoulder. "I think we should take a look at the city," she suggested.

I looked at the small group in conference, Sa'ad holding the Staff of the Phoenix as if it were his own staff of office.

"We may as well," I said, and Assumpta, Valparaiso, Digger, Omar and I all turned from the mountain-top and returned to the palace complex. No one followed us or called us back.

For a while, we followed the passages and passed through one room after another until we emerged into the daylight on one of the terraces.

This was the top level, where the most magnificent of the houses had been built. The sun beat down upon us, but the branches and leaves of the trees that grew at the roadside let only a speckled light fall upon us. Some of the trees had actually broken up the paving stones. It was like the city of Xulamqamtun, which Ari and I had explored in Mexico a few years previously—the highly civilized walls, the forest encroaching upon it with muscular remorselessness.

Entering one of the houses, we admired its mosaic floor; the roof above us had survived, but in other houses, the roofs had collapsed. Some of them had gardens, overgrown now, from which we were given a magnificent view of the oasis. From here, we could see a little more of the domed building on the island. There seemed to be white pillars holding the dome up.

The steps that led down to the next terrace were broken up by ferns and bushes and trees, so that they gave little advantage to one who went down them, except shade.

Halfway down, we found a little shrine. A statue of a woman with a child stood in it, vines creeping over her. Her foot was placed firmly on the head of a serpent.

"It's the Blessed Virgin!" I cried.

"Mother Miriam!" exclaimed Omar in delight.

Assumpta, Digger and I went down on our knees and prayed a Hail Mary; Omar, with some hesitation, followed suit. When we made the Sign of the Cross at the end, Valparaiso clumsily copied us.

"This must have been put here by Bohemund, or one of his ancestors," Assumpta said. "It's beautiful!"

We all turned to descend the rest of the steps; but as we did so, a massive explosion shook the ground beneath our feet, and we were thrown to the ground.

"Starve the lizards!" yelled Digger.

We scattered, taking cover behind what we could find. Seconds later, the whole area was pelted with bits of rock. They were mostly intercepted by the leaves above us, but some of them pattered on the ground all around us. A few severed twigs and leaves spiraled down through the bright air.

I picked myself up and stared up the mountain. A mushroom-shaped cloud was unfurling from the top into the blue sky. It widened as it rose and began to disperse.

"Sa'ad!" I said. "I told him not to do anything with the Staff of the Phoenix. Look at that!"

"He's a sheikh," Assumpta observed. "He may not feel bound by you at all."

Fuming, I stormed off up the steps, retracing as fast as I could the route we had taken to get to the little Marian shrine. The others followed me at a distance as I once more entered the ruins of the mountain palace. A few turns brought me to the steps up to the mountaintop.

Sa'ad sat, dazed, staring at a massive crater, the lip of which was inches from his outstretched feet. His face had been blackened, his hair stood out stiff, like beams of dark light. He still held the Staff of the Phoenix. Beside him, equally dazed, sat Metwallah. Sa'ad's sons and bodyguard stood at some distance, shocked and bewildered.

"What did you do, Sa'ad?" I demanded.

The sheikh made a gesture with his hand. "You can see, Cracken-bey. I made a hole in the mountain with this Staff." His eyes flashed as he looked up at me. "Think what I can do to the Romans now! I and I alone will drive them back into the sea. All this land will be mine. Caliphs will kiss the floor before my feet!"

Sa'ad glanced at Metwallah and then back at me. "Metwallah bu Jaghbub comes with a message, Cracken-bey. The Romans will be here when the sun stands highest in the sky. There are a thousand of them left—he has killed many, but many more have run away. By tomorrow at this hour, there will be none of them left at all." His eyes were on fire, his fingers clenched, white-knuckled, about the Staff of the Phoenix. "No one but I shall kill them, and I shall kill them all!"

I could see there was no point in chastising him, and backed slowly away from a madman.

"Blimey," Digger said quietly, "he's totally off his rocker."

"He wasn't like this when we first met him," I said quietly.

"I've seen this over and over," Valparaiso said. "A guy gets a sniff of power, and it smells good to him. Before you know it, there ain't no other smell for him. Just the one, and everything about him smells the same way or he don't want it."

Beyond the rim of the crater, I could see the jagged line of the mountains with the line of dunes beyond it. The last rays of the sun were just touching their very tops and, as I watched, the gold was extinguished, and our shadows stretched, long, dark, razor-edged, before us.

"Assumpta," I said, "could I have a word with you, please?"

Chapter 15
The Sun on the Dunes

It was the dark of the moon that night, but that hardly mattered, because the stars shone with a brighter light, steadier than a surgeon's hand, out here and hundreds of miles from street lights and without any humidity to waver them. The gold of the dunes had been turned by night's magic into silver. Picking up a handful of sand, I let it run through my fingers. It looked like a waterfall of silver.

I sat on the dune opposite the twin peaks that guarded the wadi that led to the City of Zerzura. Bright they were, but the stars shed no warmth on me, and I had donned an extra layer of clothes to keep me warm. Even so, I was forced to rub my hands together periodically. I couldn't risk a fire.

To my shock, a deep, eerie humming broke out all around me, as if the dunes themselves were worshiping the stars. Then I remembered the Singing Sands I had heard when we had just entered the desert—it seemed months ago, but it was really only a couple of weeks. And turning without getting up, I found as I expected Assumpta sliding down the dune from above me.

"Sorry," she said, "I forgot about that. If I'd been that careless in the Mojave, I wouldn't have gotten away with the Carnegie Diamonds."

"I never heard that they went missing."

She shrugged. "I gave them back—or left them where they could be found, at least."

I gave a quiet laugh. "Perhaps you should think of going straight."

A small grimace. "But an honest life is so dull. And I don't do any harm."

We didn't have time to go into the theology of it. "Did you get it?" I asked.

She put out one hand, palm-upwards, and reached into the folds of her coat to draw out something that glinted gold in the starlight. The Staff of the Phoenix and the Fire Stone. "Simple," she said. "As security systems go, a couple of snoring Bedouins don't take a lot to beat."

I took the Fire Stone, and held it up so that the spears of light from above pierced its heart and danced in motes, like glimmering snowflakes. I could almost feel the power within it, like an electrical surge. I had felt something like it once before, on the slopes of a northern mountain in Canada, when I had been recovering some wolframite for a Serbian inventor named Nicola Tesla.

I looked up at the crest of the dune behind us, then at the peaks on the far side of the valley. Snapping the orichalcum into the Staff of the Phoenix, I thrust it into the sand, adjusted its height and the aperture on the front, and made a few tiny adjustments to its orientation and angle.

I looked up at Assumpta. "That should do it. Now, let's not make the sand sing on the way back down."

* * *

The scout scrambled down the rough slope to join us at our position overlooking the wadi. It was early the next morning, that part of the day that's often called Nautical Twilight, when the sky is lightening but the sun has not yet become visible. The shadows below us were deep.

Sa'ad greeted the scout and they began an intense conversation.

I looked down the cliff at the floor of the wadi. Nothing stirred in the blue shadows below, but I knew that two hundred Senussi were stationed behind rocks and trees in the cliffs. Each bore a rifle.

But the real work, Sa'ad knew, would be done by the Staff of the Phoenix. Fortunately, he hadn't sent his son for it yet.

I had not slept after I had returned to the tent I shared with Digger. I had wrestled all night with my decision. It was as if another presence was in the tent with me, in addition to the snoring Australian; and it whispered doubts and slanders into my ear.

I know it seems strange. After all, people who know me know about my adventures. They seem to think I'm brave. It's true that I don't think of the danger much when I'm flying or shooting it out with some villain. But I had the option, that night, of going back on my decision. And that's what scared me.

"What are they saying, Omar?" I asked.

He listened for a moment longer, his eyes slightly narrowed. "The scout says the Romans will be here in about two hours."

"And the plan," I said quietly, looking back down the cliff, "is to lure them along the wadi to this spot, then wipe them out."

"I hope you're looking forward to this, pal," said Valparaiso, jabbing at Omar with his unlit cigarette.

Omar's eyes remained steady. He cradled his Martini-Henry. "Cracken," he said, "you know my heart. I love my family, though I do not always approve of what they do."

"You love your family?" I said. And I love mine, I thought. If I was true to the course of action I'd chosen, it was entirely possible I'd never see them again on earth.

"You know I do, effendim." Omar grinned. "Even if I cannot say what it is, I know what is here." He pounded his chest. Some of the desert rose in a faint cloud from his jerd.

"To love," I said, recalling my catechism class, "is to actively will the best for the other."

Omar gave a nod, his nostrils flaring slightly as he took in a deep breath. "I do not love this choice of my sheikh's, but then I do not love the choice the Romans have made to be here, in the land that belonged to my clan in the time of my great-grandfather's great-grandfather. Whatever my heart tells me, I must fight in this battle."

"If there is a God," Valparaiso said, "He wants us to make the hard calls. He's the harsh lieutenant in the district, who wants his cops to make their decisions in the moment. If they make the wrong choice, they could go to jail, or worse. But the Law means that they have to make the choice. It ain't easy, but it's life."

"I think you've got that wrong, Valparaiso," I answered him. Looking at my watch, I saw it was almost sunrise. The sun would be at about thirty or thirty-two degrees at this time.

I still had time. In a moment, you can make and reverse an infinite number of decisions. Only the angels don't have that luxury.

My stomach felt hollow.

Valparaiso was speaking. "I don't see no way out of this situation without spilling blood, McCracken. Do you?"

"God's not like you think He is, Valparaiso," I told him. "He never gives us a no-win situation."

It was just theology. My brain knew it was true but that didn't help my heart.

At that moment, there was an explosion, way off down the wadi. We all looked up in shock, Sa'ad whirling around and emitting a stream of Arabic.

"The Romans!" exclaimed Omar. "They are here already!"

A cloud of smoke rose into the clear blue sky, and almost at once dissipated. My mouth was dry.

Another explosion came; we could feel the shock vibrating the ground. This time, the explosion was followed by a faint roar, like heavy things falling. One or two Senussi heads poked out from hiding.

Sa'ad yelled at the scout, who scampered off the way he had come, between the rocks. Turning to one of his sons, he yelled something else, and the son dashed off into the city.

"Sheikh Sa'ad bu Jibrin says the Romans are here early, and that is their artillery. He has sent Ali for the Staff of the Phoenix."

"That didn't sound like artillery to me," said Digger, cupping his hand over his eyes and peering towards where the explosions had come from. "No report from the guns, no sound of shells flying through the air. And two shots? No artillery major would end a salvo with only two shots."

"Unless that was all he needed," I pointed out softly. I had to choke the words out, my mouth was so dry.

Sa'ad, his face like thunder, swept down the path and back through the Gates of Zerzura. We followed him. I stumbled a little on the way down. Tamarisk trees caught on my trousers or I nudged a boulder. I felt like I was a blind man walking through a brightly lit landscape.

A few minutes later, we stood outside the gates. Sa'ad's men brought us horses and we mounted, galloping off along the wadi. No more explosions came, just the echoing of our hoofbeats. The walls of the wadi flashed past, blue and red and yellow, and the air was cool on my face.

"Lord," I prayed, "if I can somehow get out of this, I'd be very grateful."

We reached the tunnel that led out into the desert, and there we threw ourselves from our mounts. Dust still unfurled slowly from the mouth of the tunnel.

Someone handed Sa'ad a torch and, following him, we all entered the tunnel.

There was no light at the end of it.

I thought about the voice last night, that I'd heard in the darkness of the tent.

"Lord," I prayed again, "keep that voice out of my ears!"

"Be brave," a Voice replied, "father of Archimedes and Rosamund McCracken." And the Voice brought with it a deep calm, a peace that folded me in its warm, comforting embrace.

Sa'ad raised the torch and examined what had happened. The tunnel was blocked by a rockfall, just like the ones we had seen inside the City of Zerzura. A few of us coughed—the air was thick with rock dust.

I joined Sa'ad in examining the wreckage. It was impassable.

"What has done this?" demanded Sa'ad. "Can Roman guns do this? And *why* would they do this? Now *they* cannot come to Zerzura, *they* cannot find the Staff of Zerzura!"

"Artillery couldn't have done this, cobber," said Digger. "It looks like . . . "

At this point, another torch flickered in the tunnel. A moment later, Ali hurried up and spoke with Sa'ad.

The Sheikh of Wadi Buma raised his hands to his head and pulled at his hair. "The Staff of Zerzura had disappeared!" he snarled. He stormed out of the tunnel and into the air.

"There has been treachery!" he ranted, "the greatest treachery the world has seen!" Turning on me, he said in low, even tones, "There will be those who will dread the moment they chose to betray the Sheikh of Wadi Buma."

I cleared my throat. "Can't you plan a new ambush for the Italians?" I asked innocently.

"It is too late," moaned Sa'ad. "Even Mohammed could not achieve such a victory. My men cannot move to new positions so fast. And we would need a new plan. Someone has stolen this victory from me." His lament turned to a snarl. "And whoever it is will pay with his blood!" He paused a moment, and a light flashed in his eyes. "But there is hope—I still have the Fire Stone!"

Reaching into his jerd, he took out a small goatskin pouch, untied the neck and took something out of it.

It was a rock, yellow as the sands around it.

Sa'ad's features froze and he glared at me. "Is this your doing?" he demanded.

But then something else caught his attention, and he took out of the pouch a square of paper, on which was a red wax seal. I couldn't see clearly, but I knew what image was in the wax—a Welsh dragon. I glanced quickly about the wadi. Assumpta was not there.

I swallowed. I could feel the peace dissipating, to be replaced by apprehension, anxiety. Perhaps the blame could fall on her, I thought. A small lie, a break in my resolve, could settle everything. After all, she was a thief, even if she was a good thief. She would understand. I was a father. I had to return to my family. Didn't that justify a small lie?

Sa'ad held out the letter to Omar. "What does this say?" he asked.

Omar read the English: "The Jewel." Valparaiso snorted out a laugh.

Sa'ad's nostrils widened and his eyes became glaring slits. "The Jewel—it is the Jewel that is lost.

And whoever stole it, his blood will run into the sands, and jackals will feast upon his corpse!"

Assumpta would understand, I thought. It wasn't cowardice. It was prudence.

But, the Voice reminded me, Archie thought I was brave.

"I did it, Sa'ad!" I cried. The sheikh turned to me, his hand now upon the hilt of his scimitar. "I placed the Staff of the Phoenix and the Fire Stone upon the dune so that, when the sun rose, its beams would blast the rocks to pieces. I calculated the angle so that the debris would block up the wadi and the Italians wouldn't be able to get to Zerzura. They might not even know anything was here! I did it, Sa'ad—let your anger fall upon me." I went down on my knees, bowing my head.

"Why wouldst thou do such a thing?" Sa'ad demanded. "These invaders are nothing to thee." He slid the scimitar from its sheath. "These dogs are invaders," he said with quiet danger. "Thou hast betrayed me."

"If you wish," I told him, without looking up, "you can kill me instead of these Italians."

The hand moved, and I saw, out of the corner of my eye, the bright blade flashing upwards. I still did not look into Sa'ad's face. "Is this the way of a Christian?" Sa'ad asked. "To betray a host and a friend?"

"No!" This time, the voice belonged to Omar. Sa'ad rounded on him, and his automatic reaction was to cringe before his sheikh, but he steeled himself, thrust out his chest, and stood his ground. "May Allah preserve Sheikh Sa'ad bu Jibrin of Wadi Buma, but would he have the blood of innocent men on his hands when he stands in the great assembly? When the scroll of his deeds is unrolled, would he hear those deeds of his given by the left hand or the right? El Cracken would guide him to the deeds of the right hand. That is a righteous deed, O Sa'ad bu Jibrin! Consider rightly. Ever was it thy custom to weigh the just against the unjust before passing thy judgments. Be constant in thy virtue, O Sheikh of Wadi Buma!"

I had not yet raised my eyes, which were fixed on Sa'ad's feet, so I could see nothing of his expression as he considered Omar's words. I waited, my mouth dry as the desert all around us, with the sheikh's shadow across me.

At last, there came a small sound, almost like a laugh, from above me. "Thy ways, O Cracken, are not my ways. Hast thou in truth such love for these Romans?"

Finally, I looked up into his face. There was wonder in his eyes, though a little caginess too. I said, "Sometimes, O Sheikh, it is easier to love a man than to like him."

A crease deepened between Sa'ad's eyes. "Your words are dark to me."

Now it was Omar who laughed. "But not to me, Sa'ad bu Jibrin. I think, O Cracken, I begin to see."

Sa'ad gave a sigh. "Well," he said, "I will spare your life. But look thou cross me never again. Thou shalt not find me so generous in my love a second time." His hand dropped and he slid the scimitar back into its sheath. "Come, we should return to Wadi Buma. It may take many days to find a way through the mountains, now this pass has been sealed up, but to one who has a will, Allah will open the way."

I started to get to my feet, but found I was being helped up by Omar. His eyes slid sideways to make sure Sa'ad was out of earshot and said, "You came very close to death there, effendim."

Making the Sign of the Cross, I replied, "I thought so too, Omar."

Omar held out his hand, and I clasped it—one of those old-fashioned handshakes where each person grasps the forearm of the other. "Where you go, I go, El Cracken," he said, "if you will have me."

"Of course!" I blurted out; but within, I thought: How will Fritz react to that?

"So, McCracken." Valparaiso sauntered up to us, a smile hinting that it might play over his lips. "I guess you had Miss Bevan steal the orichalcum. Was that her calling card in Sa'ad's pocket?"

"It was."

"Where is she now?"

"Back in Zerzura," I told him.

"Did she promise she'd stay there when we left?" I shook my head. "Then she's long gone." He gave a laugh and passed a hand over his brow. "They won't believe this back in Chicago—that I had a chance to bring in this dame and blew it."

"Then what will you tell them?"

He shrugged. "The truth. I'm going to have to think about how I sell this particular number. I'll have to make a song and dance out of some parts, put some others upstage left and hope no one notices."

Digger threw his hat upon the ground and stomped up to us. "We're going to have a pig's . . . er . . . ear of a time getting the lorry over this landslide," he said, "sorry about the language."

One by one we remounted and walked our horses back to Zerzura. On passing through the gates, I heard my name called out and Ali passed an envelope up to me.

We dismounted and the others crowded around me as I broke the seal and read Assumpta's letter.

> My Dear McCracken, and Mr. Valparaiso, Mr. Dawkins, and Omar (who I'm sure are reading this letter over your shoulder),
>
> Pardon me for deserting my post at a time of danger, but I've decided to switch armies—I'm joining the Italians to see if they can help me back to Benghazi, and from

there, who knows? Hong Kong, perhaps, or perhaps Melbourne, where I might dabble in art, particularly Foxes, which might be popular in the future.

"Hey," interjected Digger, "I got pals she can bunk with there!"

"Why would foxes be popular in the future?" wondered Valparaiso.

I read on:

I went back to try and find the Staff of the Phoenix and the Fire Stone, but they were both gone. Perhaps buried in the sand—the force of the explosion must have been pretty strong.

Once again, Mac, I've thoroughly enjoyed this adventure, and look forward to the next one. Please pass on my love to Ari and Rose, and particularly to that mischievous little man Archie.

Yours,
Assumpta Bevan,
a.k.a. Ramona Fortescue.

"The Staff of the Phoenix is gone!" I gasped.

"You think she took it?" wondered Digger.

Valparaiso shook his head. "That's not the way she operates," he observed. "She steals something for the thrill, then gives it back. She couldn't give that thing back. It don't make sense. It must be like she said—the Staff got buried in the dune. We could go looking for it, but it would be like searching for a pebble on a beach."

"So what's the next step?" wondered Digger.

"Back to Wadi Buma," I said, "to pick up Barbs, then if Sa'ad can help us get to Benghazi, maybe we can get passage to Cairo. Maybe Sikorsky has turned up with the LS3 by now. Then—Australia, Digger. We'll take you home."

"Bonzer," remarked Digger.

"Would you like to come with us, Mr. Valparaiso?" I asked.

Valparaiso held up his unlit cigarette. "Well, that would be sweet, now, wouldn't it? But I got my job to do—I got to track down that female jewel thief. I caught her once, and I can catch her again, I guess." Dropping his cigarette, he ground it out on the dusty ground. "I guess she's wise to me now, so it's going to be a little tougher." He winked. "But it's sure going to be fun."

Chapter 16
A Dirigible Solution

While Sa'ad sent out scouts to find the best way back to the Jebel Akhdar, Digger, Valparaiso and I explored the city a little further. We had already seen the topmost terrace, and now we went down the steps again, past the shrine of Our Lady, until we reached the next terrace.

On this level, we found a wide variety of temples. Some of them were nothing more than roofs supported by pillars, with statues inside of strange figures, half-man and half-beast. Others were enclosed, with stained altars. There were some inscriptions, written in the strange script Ari had deciphered, but of course we could make nothing of them. We found a mosque and a Christian church, with crosses on it that looked like the ones we had seen in the Temple of Isis.

Through it all, the animals wandered freely. For a few minutes, we stopped to watch an okapi chewing at the grass within the walls of an open-air shrine. He was no more than a yard away from us and, when we first arrived, he looked up incuriously at us but then went back to his meal. More parrots swung from tree to tree, and we saw monkeys who chattered angrily at us as we passed. And there were cats and other domesticated animals too. We saw a herd of cows in one open field, all happily chewing the cud.

"These Zerzurans don't seem to have lacked much," Valparaiso observed. "All you can eat, on the hoof or on the trees."

"And I saw cotton plants this morning, on the other side of the lake," Digger pointed out.

The trees were thick further down the side of the mountain, but we picked our way through the deep forest until we reached another terrace. Here, between the tree-trunks were the ruins of the poorer sort of houses. We found the road, much disrupted by the roots of the trees, and followed it a little way, enjoying the cooler air beneath the green canopy. Once, the road widened out into a square, which must have been a market or bazaar in the days of Zerzura's prosperity. We found large clay pots here, mostly broken, all damaged in one way or another. One of them held an unpleasant tenant—a Desert Horned Viper, a pale face lurking in the shadows, with slit eyes and horns protruding from behind them. Digger advised us against making a closer acquaintance.

Walking on, we found the open mouth of what looked like a mine. I could make out absolutely nothing inside, it was so dark. But Valparaiso stooped and picked something out of the dirt. Blowing the dirt off this small object, he held it up for us all to see.

"Orichalcum!" I exclaimed. Casting about at our feet, we were quickly able to find several more, although none of them was the size my own had been.

"So they used to mine these things," commented Valparaiso. "I might have guessed it. I guess that's how they got so rich." He gave a lop-sided grin. "Better fill your pockets!"

I looked down at the small mound of red gems in the palm of my hand. "I'm glad the Italians didn't find this place," I said. Returning my gaze to the mine entrance, I added, "But I don't think Sa'ad ought to get it, either."

"What's on your mind, Mac?" asked Valparaiso.

I ushered them away from the mine entrance, taking my electric torch from my pocket and unscrewing the end. Touching the battery to one of the Fire Stones, I sent a lance of red light out towards the mine. It struck right over the lintel. The three of us ducked as the rocks split apart and cascaded down into the mouth of the mine. Two more strikes from the orichalcum beam, and the mine was completely concealed.

"Shall we go?" I asked, returning the torch to my pocket.

Down on the bottom level of Zerzura were all the public buildings—baths like in a Roman city, gardens, a theatre and a stadium. The lake in the middle was a shimmering azure and a small herd of zebras grazed on its shore. They were totally unafraid of us, and merely lifted their heads in curiosity as we passed.

"This is a lovely place," Digger observed, "almost like Oz. I reckon me and the missus could settle down here. It's a bit thin on neighbours, mind you. A bloke could get a bit lonely after ten years or so."

Suddenly, ahead of us and closer to the shore of the lake, a great flame rose through the trees. We all gasped. It wasn't an explosion, just a surge of fire. And silhouetted against the momentary blaze was the shape of a man.

"Omar?" I said, and we all ran forward.

By the time we reached him, the fire had gone completely. Omar had been knocked off his feet. His beard and clothes were singed, and smouldered slightly. Before him was an almost perfect circle of burned grass. In the centre was a small pile of grey ashes.

"Omar, what happened?" I asked.

Omar shook his head. "I do not rightly know, effendim," he said. "I was strolling about this most admirable and beautiful place, when suddenly I felt a burning against my chest. It was the egg, effendim—remember, the egg I took from the throne room. It had begun to burn so hot I could not hold it. I dropped it, and when it struck the ground, that great fire you saw erupted from it." His eyes opened wide and he pointed.

A small downy head with a curved beak had emerged from the pile of ashes.

Omar scrambled through the burned grass and reached out to the fledgling. Tenderly, he took it into the palm of his hand. Stretching its beak wide, the phoenix gave a little squeak.

"It is quite cool to the touch," he observed, "now."

"What are you going to do with it?" wondered Digger.

Omar shrugged. "I cannot say. By its nature, a phoenix could never have a mother. So how does it learn to eat? What does it eat? Its mother—or father—survived in Zerzura all its life, however long that might be. So this beast can presumably teach itself to eat. Perhaps I should leave it here."

Omar set the phoenix on the ground, and we all turned away and began to walk.

We had not gone five paces, when a squeaking broke out behind us. The phoenix had followed us with hurried steps, squeaking all the way.

"Well, look at that," said Valparaiso, "I guess one of us is his Pop."

Crouching, Omar held out his hand, and the phoenix hopped up onto his palm, where it squatted and tucked its head under its wing.

Before we could go another step, however, Omar looked up. He held up his hand as if to still a conversation, and cocked his head.

"What can you hear, Omar?" I asked in a whisper.

But before he could answer, I heard it too: a low mechanical buzzing sound.

Digger said, "I think they're engines."

My heart soared suddenly. "Mercedes engines!" I cried; and even as I said it, the snub nose of an airship appeared between the leaves overhead. I began to laugh. "Sikorsky!" I said, "you crazy old Ukrainian! You made it at last!"

We all dashed out from under the trees and waved and shouted like mad. It was about two hundred feet from the ground, and the gondola was directly over our heads. As it moved on, we saw the curved windows in the stern, where the dining room, or *Speiseraum*, as Fritz called it, was located.

At once, the engines cut, a rope ladder unfurled from the door of the gondola, and a lithe figure slid to the ground.

A moment later, Ari threw herself into my arms.

"I should have known you'd find us!" I cried.

"A blind man could have followed your trail through the desert," Ari answered. "We picked up the truck you lost. You took a long detour north."

"Well, that was because . . . "

Ari smiled. "I know."

Looking up, I saw that another figure had appeared in the doorway and was making its way more cautiously down the ladder.

Digger started forward. "Barbs?" he said.

Barbs gave a start and accidentally let go of the rope ladder, but Digger was there to catch her.

"Don't worry, old girl—I got you. Give us a pash!" Setting her on her feet, they kissed so that there was an audible smack upon their releasing one another.

"Now, don't you go walkabouts on me no more!" complained Barbs.

"Bloody oath, sheila!" replied Digger incomprehensibly. "I won't let you go again, that's dinkum." He grinned. "Death can't part us now!"

"Well, it didn't last time," answered Barbs.

Ari jabbed her thumb up at the LS3. "You'd better come on up," she suggested. "We've got quite a full ark."

I snaked up the ladder and found hands willing to haul me through the doorway and into the gondola. They belonged to my good friend, Nicolas Jaubert, the French diver, who instantly clapped me in an embrace and kissed me in that Gallic way on either cheek.

"*Bonjour*, McCracken! Together again, *oui*? Now the adventures, they will commence *vraiment*!"

"Jaubert! Good to see you! Give me a little time before the next adventure, though, would you? How did you get here?"

Jaubert spread his hands. "It was the Ukrainian—he picked me up from Brittany before coming here. I have nothing else to do right now. The world is very quiet now the war is over. So I think, why not see the McCrackens once more? Life is more exciting when we are together, *non*?"

Archie ran into my arms, and Rose reached out to me from Fritz's arms. "Dad, you should see this thing!" shouted Archie. "It's the bee's feet!"

"I think you mean the *bee's knees*. Are you talking about the airship? Fritz, how are you? And how is your family?"

"They are here, Herr McCracken. I would like to introduce to you Helga, my wife."

A pretty petite lady in a dirndl standing beside Fritz dropped a curtsey.

"Frau Bauer," I said, "it's wonderful to meet you at last."

Helga looked confused, and Fritz explained, "She has not, Herr McCracken, yet had the opportunity much English to learn. But she will learn."

In the distance, I could hear sounds to which I was unaccustomed on the LS3: children playing. I couldn't make out the language at all, but I guessed at a mixture of Italian and German. Fritz grinned with pride. "My family, Herr McCracken—they are all here: Helmut and all of them. You have met Helmut already, I believe."

I nodded. "All thirteen of them?"

"Fourteen, Herr McCracken," Fritz corrected me.

"Dad," insisted Archie, "you have to see this thing."

"The airship?"

Archie nodded vigorously. "It has a kitchen, and a car, and tables and beds. And I saw some guns too, though Mom didn't let me touch them. We flew over the desert, and then over some mountains, and saw some deer and stuff!"

"Actually, I've seen it before," I said, "and so have you, though you don't remember . . . "

At that moment, a stream of urchins ran along the corridor towards the *Speiseraum*, pursued by Maria and Serpe, who each gave me a cheery wave in passing.

"Dad!" A pair of hands forcibly turned my head to face their owner.

"Okay, Archie," I said, "you can show me around. Can we start with the wheelhouse?"

"Yeah!" Archie slid down to the floor, I took Rose and followed him forward, past the radio room and into the wide space of glass and polished steel, gears and wheels, which was the nerve-centre of the LS3.

The blond-haired Ukrainian, Vassily Sikorsky, greeted me as Jaubert had done.

"*Dobro pazhalovat!*" he exclaimed. "Welcome aboard, McCracken!"

"Thank you, Sikorsky. Nice beard—it suits you."

Helmut, Fritz's eldest son, who had evidently been acting as First Mate, snapped his heels on seeing me and gave me a curt bow, which I returned.

Sikorsky returned to the wheel and pulled back on the elevators. The LS3's nose tipped upwards.

"Now everyone is here, *da*? Even my Mother and my sister, Katerina Ilyovna Sikorsky, but you may call her Katya."

Something brushed against my leg, and I looked down.

"Even Edison's here," I said, reaching down to scratch our cat behind the ear.

Sikorsky eased back on the throttles, and the engines thrummed higher and higher as the LS3 rose above the lost oasis. Below us, I could see Sa'ad organizing his men for the return to Jebel Akhdar—the scouts had evidently found a way through the mountains. They all looked up, screwing their eyes against the brilliant sky, as we flew over them.

"Do you think we should tell them we have a ride out of here, Sport?" wondered Digger.

Valparaiso shook his head. "They've figured it out by now."

"In any case, effendim," said Omar, "there may not be space for them in this flying ship." His face was pale, and I realized that he had probably never flown before.

"Fritz," I said, "could you show Omar around the ship. Perhaps you could particularly show him the galley?"

"*Jawohl*, Herr McCracken!"

I felt Ari's arm slip around my waist, while Rose rested her head on my shoulder and Archie danced around the wheelhouse, showing me all the dials and wheels and cogs and explaining what they did.

It was good to be home.

* * *

Some hours later, the LS3 flew in eastwards, and a quiet had descended upon the gondola as Fritz and Helga, Serpe and Maria, and Ari and I had put all the smaller children to bed. Archie snored softly beneath the porthole that showed the purple desert sky, pricked by the first of the stars. Ari lowered Rose into her crib and relaxed into an easy chair opposite me.

"So," she said, "there are still some things I don't understand. The orichalcum, for example."

"I think it must have got lost in the sands," I answered, whispering so as not to awaken the children. "Sa'ad couldn't find it, or the Staff of the Phoenix."

"That's not what I mean. Where did it come from? We thought Vassily had found it, here on the LS3, but he says he didn't."

I frowned. "Well, that's puzzling," I said. "I thought it was lost, then it turns up and no one knows where it came from. Maybe it wasn't really lost. There has to be a natural explanation."

"Perhaps. But then there's also Brother Osvaldo."

"What about him?"

"Well, other than Assumpta, none of us has seen him. Fr. Murphy says no one at the dig knew him, and the Jesuits back in Rome couldn't identify him."

"So, he was an imposter," I said, feeling a shiver go up my spine. "I don't like that—I don't like not being able to explain things. I don't like adventures with loose ends." I stared out of the window at the cold stars. "Perhaps we should go back to Zerzura."

"I'd like that, one day," replied Ari. "But not now—we have to take Digger and Barbs to Australia. We have Zerzura's coordinates. We can go back whenever we want to."

"Right, so we can come back after the wedding and try to tie up some of these loose ends." I picked up a newspaper from the night-stand and scanned the front cover. "What's been happening while I've been in the desert?" I asked.

"Well, in America Congress passed a Prohibition Act," said Ari.

"What does that mean?" I asked. American politics has always been a mystery to me.

"It means selling alcohol is illegal."

"What a stupid idea."

"The President thought so too; he vetoed it, but Congress went over his veto and passed it anyway."

"We'd better not go to America any time soon," I said. "If they'll do that, who knows what idiocy they'll get up to next?" I tossed the newspaper back onto the night-stand. "The world's become a crazy place, what with Communists and prohibitionists and people imitating Italian priests."

Ari nodded. "Well," she said, "this adventure is over for the time being, and we don't have prohibition on the LS3." Rising from her seat, she held out her hand to me. "Come on," she said, "I'll get you a whisky."

THE END

Kofta

Ingredients

1 lb. ground beef
1 onion, finely chopped
1 egg yolk
1 tbs. oregano
2 tsp. salt
1 tsp. pepper

Directions

1. Chop onion finely, in a food processor if possible
2. Mix together the ground beef, onion, egg yolk, oregano, salt and pepper.
3. Shape into two sausages about eight inches long.
4. Either broil for 10 minutes, flip, and then broil the other side for 10 minutes, or grill over a medium-high heat, turning every five minutes for 10-12 minutes. They should be blackened.

Egyptian Green Beans with Carrots

Ingredients

1 tbs. vegetable oil
1 large onion, chopped
2 tbs. tomato paste
2 cloves garlic, minced
2 cups chicken broth
¼ tsp. ground cardamom
1 bay leaf
2 tsp. salt
1 tsp pepper
8 oz. green beans
8 oz. sliced carrots
Couscous or rice

Directions

1. Heat oil in a pot over a medium heat.
2. Add onion and stir until translucent, 6-8 minutes.
3. Add garlic and cook for 2 minutes.
4. Stir in tomato paste and cook for 1 minute.
5. Add chicken stock, cardamom, bay leaf, salt and pepper. Bring to a boil.
6. Add green beans and carrots and return to a boil.
7. Reduce heat to medium-low and simmer about 30 minutes, or until green beans and carrots are softened.
8. Serve over couscous or rice.

Dukka

Ingredients

⅔ cup chopped almonds
2 tbs. sesame seeds
4 tsp. red chile powder
2 tsp. turmeric
1 tsp. celery salt
1 tsp. cumin seeds
1 tsp. coriander
1 tsp. onion salt

Directions

Place all ingredients into a food processor and blend until they form a fine powder. This is mostly for the almonds necessary.

About the Author

Like the famous Cat, Mark Adderley was born in Cheshire, England. His early influences included C. S. Lewis and adventure books of various kinds, and his teacher once wrote on his report card, "He should go in for being an author," advice that stuck with him. He studied for some years at the University of Wales, where he became interested in medieval literature, particularly the legend of King Arthur. But it was in graduate school that he met a clever and beautiful American woman, whom he moved to the United States to marry. He spent some time as a professor of literature, and is now the Director of Religious Education at the St. Thomas More Newman Center at the University of South Dakota. He is the author of a number of novels about King Arthur for adults, and originally wrote the McCracken books for his younger two children.

Made in the USA
Columbia, SC
02 July 2021